TRAVIS

Jim Travis had every penny of his hard-earned savings in Sweetwater's bank. It was his future — but when Luke Parsons and his wild bunch cleaned out the town's bank, Jim's money was part of the haul. With no help from the town, Jim rode out to retrieve his money, trailing the Parsons bunch across wild territory. Parsons threw everything he had at the lone rider dogging his heels, yet Jim kept on coming — and forced a final, savage showdown.

RICHARD WYLER

◆

TRAVIS

Complete and Unabridged

LINFORD
Leicester

First published in Great Britain in 1985

First Linford Edition
published 2007

British Library CIP Data

Wyler, Richard
    Travis.—Large print ed.—
    Linford western library
    1. Western stories
    2. Large type books
    I. Title
    823.9'14 [F]

    ISBN 978–1–84617–855–9

Published by
F. A. Thorpe (Publishing)
Anstey, Leicestershire

Set by Words & Graphics Ltd.
Anstey, Leicestershire
Printed and bound in Great Britain by
T. J. International Ltd., Padstow, Cornwall

This book is printed on acid-free paper

Dedicated to the memory of Peter Watts. A good and true friend who will be missed by all who were lucky enough to have known him.

1

It started out as a pretty ordinary day. Midweek. Fairly quiet. One of those days that generally slips by without much happening to break the routine. Sweetwater was one of those towns that had existed long enough to have evolved ritualized patterns. They carried the town from day to day with little to intrude on those patterns.

By mid-morning the initial activity had pretty well slackened off. Sweetwater's main street was almost deserted. A few horses stood listlessly at the hitch rail outside the town's single saloon. There were always a few individuals with the inclination to have a drink even at such an early time of the day.

A dry wind was drifting in off the flats that lay to the south of town. There wasn't much out in that direction except for a wide tract of dry land dotted with scrub oak and cactus. The wind picked up fine, gritty dust as it approached Sweetwater and rattled it against the weathered, unpainted boards of the buildings on the edge of town.

Sugden's livery was one of those buildings. The owner, Hec Sugden, a grizzled oldster who had been one of the first to put down his marker when Sweetwater was being laid out, stood at the open doors of the rambling stable. Sugden was a man who liked to stand back and watch the world go by. He was an observer of human nature, given more to listening than to talking.

He watched now as six riders moved slowly across the flats, pale wreaths of dust rising from under the hooves of their horses. The dust had long since caked men and animals alike, almost merging them with the pale backdrop of the landscape. As Sugden silently eyed the riders he jammed thick curls of tobacco into the bowl of the charred old pipe he continually smoked. He was lighting the pipe as the riders eased on by the livery, and he caught a glimpse of taut, unshaven faces beneath the brims of travel-stained hats. Puffing out thick clouds of ripe smoke he saw the riders angling up main street to rein in by the saloon.

The six riders dismounted, talking quietly amongst themselves. They took their time. Made no untoward moves.

If anyone *had* been watching closely he might have become aware of the fact that when the riders dismounted five of them passed the reins of their horses to the sixth man. He remained with his back to the hitch rail.

Two of the riders removed their rifles from the saddleboots, tucking them loosely under their arms, muzzles aimed at the ground. Yet another unhitched a pair of large saddlebags from his horse and draped them over his shoulder.

There were a few moments more of subdued talk before five of the men eased away from the hitch rail, leaving the sixth man to tend the horses. The five wandered along the street. Two of them paused at the window of Meyer's gunshop and stood looking over the wide display of weapons. After a while Meyer himself appeared in the doorway of the store and began to talk with the men. The conversation lasted for a few minutes as the merits of one gun against another were discussed, and then Meyer, smiling and bobbing his head, vanished back inside the store.

By this time the other three had strolled further uptown. They gave the impression of being nothing more than casual visitors having a look round. They could have been migrants taking a well-earned break from the rigours of the trail.

Ten — maybe fifteen — minutes drifted by. By the end of this time the five men had regrouped. They were standing in a loose bunch just outside Remsberg's Mercantile. One of them, lighting the thin cigar clenched in his teeth, raised his head to stare over the shoulder of one of his partners. His hard, unflinching gaze was fixed on the building directly across the street.

It happened to be Sweetwater's bank.

★   ★   ★

George Asher shifted restlessly on the hard wooden seat, glancing furtively at the clock on the bank wall. *A good two hours before he could go for his lunch break!* He groaned inwardly. It had been one of those tiresome mornings. Very few customers had come into the bank. And there was little to do in the bank itself. Banks were also expected to be silent, sober places, so casual chatter, even when the place was empty, was frowned upon. So Asher had filled in all the entries in his deposit book. Checked and double-checked to be certain everything was correct. He didn't want Henry Sutton to find any errors. Sutton was the president of the bank. It was his bank. In fact Sutton *was* the bank. And he insisted on keeping a personal check on the day-to-day running of the place. He was a hard man to work for. He expected total commitment and loyalty from his employees, even though there were only two of them. Asher didn't mind being worked hard. He was glad to have a job in a place like Sweetwater's bank. It was giving him experience. He was young and he was ambitious and willing to learn. Sutton himself was away on business until later in the day, and Asher was determined to show that he was capable of being in charge while Sutton was absent. The only trouble was the boredom that sometimes set in during quiet periods. If only there was some kind of diversion ... he felt a momentary rise of excitement, glancing awkwardly along the polished counter ...

Mary Brewster, an attractive girl in her early twenties — she was the other member of staff — felt Asher's eyes on her. A warm flush rose to colour her cheeks, and she pretended not to be aware of his scrutiny. Inwardly she was pleased. She liked Asher. He was of her own age, a pleasant, likeable young man, and Mary kept wishing he would do more than just peep at her when she wasn't supposed to be looking. She gave him all the encouragement she could without allowing herself to become too bold. The trouble was it didn't seem to be enough. He was a shy person, she knew, so she was either going to have to be a lot more patient, or initiate some sort of action herself. *But it would have been nice*, she thought, *if he would* . . . She almost laughed out loud at her outrageous thoughts. Her mother would have been shocked to learn what her daughter had been imagining. Mary allowed a faint smile to show. *George Asher would have been shocked too!* She sighed. Maybe one day he would do something positive. *One day!*

Glancing up from her position behind the counter Mary looked out through the bank window. It was one of those ornately decorated affairs with the bank's name emblazoned across it in fancy gilt lettering. The glass itself was layered with a fine film of dust, deposited there by the soft wind that was blowing in off the flats beyond town. Through the window Mary could see two men crossing the street. They seemed to be approaching the bank. She sat upright in case they came in. Henry Sutton expected his employees to be alert and ready to serve *all* the time.

Heavy boots thumped across the boardwalk. The blurred shapes of the two men darkened the glass of the doors. As the doors swung open and the men stepped inside, Mary glanced at Asher. She wasn't sure why. All she *was* aware of was a momentary feeling of unease. There was no reasoning behind it. The men were travel-stained and dusty, their clothing rough — but so too were many of the bank's customers. *Cowmen. Cattle buyers. Hunters.* They all used Sweetwater's bank, and few of them ever came in

8

dressed for a social evening.

'Good day, gentlemen,' Asher greeted the pair. 'Can I be of assistance?'

The taller of the two dumped a pair of empty saddlebags on the counter right under Asher's nose.

'Fill it, boy, and do it right quick!'

Asher simply stared at him. His face was blank, as if he knew what the man meant but refused to accept it.

'Do it, boy,' the man hissed through tightclenched teeth.

The doors opened again and three more men stepped inside. They had the same general appearance as the pair confronting Asher. One of them remained at the doors, closing them firmly. The others took up positions at the window.

The man who had placed the saddlebags in front of Asher deliberately removed the heavy revolver holstered on his hip. He raised the gun until the muzzle was a scant fraction of an inch from Asher's face. There was a solid, oiled double-click as the hammer was slowly dogged back.

'I were you, boy, I'd do it. Right now you are close to having your brains splashed all over the floor. So why don't you fill those bags with all the paper money in this place'.

'*For God's sake do it, George! Do what they say!*' Mary yelled suddenly. There was no doubt in her mind that these men would hurt Asher if he didn't do what they wanted.

Mary's words had more effect on Asher than the gun thrust in his face. He reached down to yank open his cash drawer. In his haste he jammed the drawer. He glanced up with a despairing expression on his pale face. Beads of sweat caught the light as he moved.

'The drawer's stuck. I can't . . . ' he began.

The man holding the revolver scowled angrily. 'You son of a bitch!' he muttered. He swung his left fist across the counter, clouting Asher across the side of the face. The sound of the blow was loud in the silent room. The impact rocked Asher's head to one side. Blood began to well out of a gash in his cheek. Stumbling away from the counter Asher fell to the floor, groaning softly.

Mary moved toward him. As she did every gun in the room swung round to cover her.

'Hell, girl, stand still!' somebody snapped.

'If you want the money I have to move,' Mary said defiantly. Inwardly she was terrified; on a practical level she knew that the best thing was to give these men what they wanted so they would leave.

One of the men at the window gave a low chuckle. 'Can't argue with the little lady on that.'

The man with the revolver glanced in Mary's direction. 'Do it, girl.'

Surprised at her own coolness Mary opened her cash drawer and took out all the banknotes. She stacked them on the counter, then moved to Asher's drawer. Working calmly she loosened the jammed drawer, then removed the money.

The man with the revolver watched as his companion packed the money away. He glanced over Mary's shoulder at the solid bulk of the massive safe that stood against the wall.

'Keys?'

Mary nodded. She crouched beside Asher's stirring form and felt in his coat pocket for the safe key.

'Hurry up, girl', the revolver man urged.

One of the other men chuckled. 'Leave her be. Maybe she's found something in there a heap more fun than his keys.'

Ignoring the remark Mary crossed to the safe and used the key to unlock it. She pulled open the thick heavy doors.

'That's what we came for,' a voice said.

'Hell, yeah!'

The revolver man banged his fist on the counter. 'We'll talk later. Right now I want those bags filled.'

Mary took the saddlebags from the counter and began to pack in the neat stacks of banknotes. By the time she had the pouches filled and the flaps buckled George Asher had recovered sufficiently to be able to climb to his feet. He leaned against the counter, his face sickly white and streaked with blood.

'Rest easy, boy, it ain't your damn money we're taking,' the revolver man said, a grin forming on his unshaven face.

Mary dumped the heavy saddlebags on the counter. Her expression was stony. 'That's all the money there is,' she said evenly.

The revolver man shoved the bulging saddlebags across to his companion. 'Let's go!'

The five men left the bank as swiftly and as silently as they had entered, leaving the door wide open. Thin swirls of dust drifted in from the street.

Through the window Mary could see a man leading six horses up to the bank. *Thank God*, she thought, *they'll be gone in a minute!* She felt the tension begin to flow out of her.

And then — for the second time that day — she heard the *click-click* of a gun being cocked.

She turned, the colour draining from her face.

'*No, George!*'

Asher ignored her. He raised the counter-flap and ran to the open door. A long-barrelled Colt .45 hung from his right fist.

'Let them go, George, please,' Mary pleaded. She caught hold of his arm at the door. 'Let them have the money!'

He glanced at her. He looked angry and scared all at the same time, and then, oddly he smiled at her.

'No,' he said. 'I can't do that.'

He shrugged off her restraining hand and stepped outside, lifting the revolver.

A man yelled.

Another cursed in a long monotone.

The thunderous crash of a gunshot filled the air.

A horse shrilled in alarm.

Then a shattering volley of shots crashed out.

George Asher's bullet riddled body fell back through the door of the bank, the still-smoking Colt slipping from his fingers. As Asher crumpled to the floor, his lifeblood staining the scuffed boards, all hell broke loose in Sweetwater.

★ ★ ★

'Jesus Christ, hold them damn horses!'

'I'm tryin'. You'd be spooked if somebody shot off a gun right next to your ass!'

The revolver man had his own mount under control. Hooking the bulging saddlebags over the saddlehorn he swung up on his horse's back, snatching up the loose reins. His features were set in a taut snarl of anger.

'Let's get the hell out of this damn town!'

Running figures burst out of the saloon down the street. A gun exploded. The bullet whined past the grouped men and shattered the bank's big window.

15

Glass flew in all directions.

One of the bank robbers turned in his saddle and loosed off a volley of shots in the direction of the saloon. The hasty shooting resulted in nothing more than structural damage to the saloon's frontage. But it also had the effect of driving the men on the porch to deeper cover.

'Let's go!' yelled the revolver man. He drove his spurs deep into his horse's sides, forcing the animal along the street in a wild, headlong gallop, the rest of his bunch following in a straggly line.

A number of guns opened up as the gang thundered up the street. The robbers returned some of the fire. Not one shot hit its intended target. The gunfire from the citizens of Sweetwater was directed at fast-moving horsemen. The robbers themselves were firing at the gallop. Both sides broke a deal of glass and splintered a lot of wood.

As the riders reached the far end of town a single figure appeared, blocking their way. A lean figure with a glittering badge pinned to his shirt. He stood his ground as the riders thundered toward him, lifting the long-barrelled revolver he was carrying.

It was the act of a brave and dedicated man. And it almost got him killed that day.

One of the riders hauled back on his reins, almost bringing his horse to the ground. He swung the rifle he was carrying across his saddle, holding for a moment before he triggered a single shot.

The bullet caught the lawman in the left leg. The impact spun him round and dumped him face down in the dirt. Blood began to soak through the leg of his pants. Aware of his exposed position the man rolled frantically to the side of the street as the approaching riders drove on by him. Coughing against the swirl of dust, and ignoring the surge of raw pain that engulfed his leg, he shoved himself to a sitting position. He lifted his revolver and began firing at the riders. He took his time, knowing the range of his weapon and its particular eccentricities. He had six shots and he used them all. He fired and cocked and fired again. On his fourth shot he was rewarded with the sight of one of the riders jerking sideways and almost leaving his saddle. The man retained his seat, hauling himself upright. There was a sudden blossoming of red on his left thigh, and the man clamped a hand to it, hunching over as he rode on.

When his gun's hammer fell on an empty chamber the lawman let it sag. He watched the distant riders cut off out over the empty flats beyond town. There was no way anyone was going to catch them now. Those riders would be heading for the foothills and the mountains beyond. If they carried on long enough they'd hit Mexico. If they did that . . . well . . .

The street began to fill with the curious and the angry and the down-right pain-in-the-asses. Somebody got round to asking the lawman if he was all right, to which fool question the lawman answered in the most direct and forthright manner possible, which did a great deal to upset some of the womenfolk present, but by that time the lawman was past caring who got upset. His day had been spoiled so he didn't see why anyone else should go home without getting a taste. He had a feeling this was going to be a long-remembered day in Sweetwater. For one thing he'd recognised a couple of the bank robbers, so at least he knew *who* had robbed the town. Not that it helped much. A lot of folk were going to be upset when they heard what had happened. The lawman, who was called Sam Tyree, had a feeling that the matter wouldn't end here. The people of Sweetwater were going to be hollering for some kind of action. It was their money that had been taken from the bank. They were going to want it back. One way and another something would have to be done . . .

* ★ * ★ * ★

Some time in the late afternoon Jim Travis crested the final ridge and took his horse across a wide meadow that was knee-deep in grass bent by the cooling breeze from the distant peaks. Jim eased his stiff body in the saddle, letting his horse pick its own way. On the far side of the meadow the timberline began, and he could see the clustered ranks of trees clinging to the higher slopes above him. On those high slopes, where the greenery gave way to naked rock, white banks of snow clung, defying the efforts of the wind to loosen it. During the next couple of days Jim knew he'd be riding that high country, doggedly following the faint trail that had already brought him this far.

The breeze caught the branches of the nearby trees. The rustling broke Jim's reverie and he took up the slack reins, guiding his horse into the timber. His nose picked up the mingled scents of the forest. The earthy smell of the thick carpet of leaf-mould. The tang of pollen drifting from some bank of wild flowers. It was good country, Jim had decided earlier, skirting a silver lake bounded by lush greenery. The kind of place where a man could put his roots down deep and build himself a fine life. The land was wide and offered everything a man could wish for. Jim had seen deer and elk, silver-flashing trout in the clear, fast flowing streams.

Now, though, his thoughts were soured by a remembrance of what had brought him this far from Sweetwater. The reason for this long trek across country. Ahead of him somewhere in the wild territory beyond the mountains were six men. The men Jim Travis was looking for. They had something belonging to Jim, and he wasn't about to quit until he had it back.

A half-hour later Jim reined in on the banks of a tumbling stream cutting through the forest. In a small clearing, surrounded by tall aspens and pines, he dismounted and unsaddled his horse.

He tethered it on a rope that allowed it access to the water, then humped his gear to a spot where he could build himself a fire. Gathering a bundle of dry timber Jim got a fire going. He took his blackened coffee pot and filled it from the stream, adding a handful of coffee beans. He set the pot in the flames. Sitting back on his heels he fished a thick chunk of salted bacon out of his sack. Before he sliced it he held it up and took a sniff; the day before he'd suspected it might be starting to get a little ripe; now, though, he wasn't so sure. He deliberated for a while, then took out his knife and cut off a couple of thick wedges. Next chance he got he'd pick up some fresh meat. Maybe shoot himself some deer meat. He took out his fry pan and wedged it over the flames on a couple of flat stones he'd picked up. Dropping the bacon in the pan he sat back and waited for his meal to cook.

Up through the canopy of green he could see fragments of the sky. Turning his head he could just make out the hazed tips of the distant peaks. To the north of the peaks he spotted a bank of dark cloud; thick and heavy, they looked fat with rain; Jim wondered if a storm was on its way. That was all he needed. A rainstorm would wipe away what little trail he had to follow. He climbed to his feet and stood for a long time, just watching those far-off clouds, yet knowing that they could sweep in pretty quick.

Standing he was tall, loose-limbed, his long legs lean and hard muscled. There wasn't an ounce of fat on his body. Beneath the faded dark shirt his shoulders hinted at a strength not initially apparent. A sweat-stained, curl-brimmed hat was pushed to the back of his head, exposing the thick mass of dark brown hair that constantly tumbled down over his forehead. His face, deeply tanned, betrayed his years. Despite the seriousness of his mood Jim's youthful appearance might have fooled many; he was twenty six years old, and whatever others might think he was no man's fool.

The aroma of frying bacon reached his nostrils. Jim dragged his gaze from the distant stormclouds and returned to reality. He crouched by the fire and used his knife to turn the slices of bacon over. That done he moved to his saddle and slid the Winchester rifle from the scuffed leather scabbard. Sitting cross-legged on the grass he stripped the rifle down, checked the action, and reassembled the weapon. When he'd completed the task he suddenly became very conscious of what he'd just done. He laid the rifle on the grass beside him. For a moment he wondered just what the hell he was doing. He was no lawman. No trained officer. He was a working cowhand. Not a man-hunter . . .

Then he remembered why he *was* here. It came back with a jolt, and Jim felt his anger rise again. As it had been doing with regularity ever since he'd heard about the raid on the Sweetwater bank. The trouble was it had been over and done with a day and a half before Jim managed to ride into Sweetwater and talk with Sheriff Tyree.

Tyree had been pretty considerate even though he was in fair pain from the bullet that had been fired through his left leg during the raid on Sweetwater's bank. Because that was what had happened. A man named Luke Parsons — an outlaw wanted throughout the territory — had brought his gang into Sweetwater, walked into the bank and out again with over 40,000 dollars. During the robbery they shot and killed one of the bank's tellers, and also shot Tyree. Yet they hadn't got away completely untouched. Despite being down in the street and losing a lot of blood, Tyree had still been able to put a bullet into one of Parsons' men. Jim had been out riding herd on a big bunch of cattle on the north pasture of the AK spread when news had reached him about the robbery. Asking one of the crew to stand in for him Jim had gone straight to the AK house and had a word with Al Keenan, the man he worked for. Then he'd ridden for Sweetwater and Sheriff Tyree's office.

'Ease off, Jim,' Tyree had said.

Jim had stood glaring up at Tyree from the street. Sweetwater's lawman was sitting in a cane-backed chair that had been placed in the bright sunlight on the boardwalk outside the jail. Tyree sat nursing his aching leg, wishing the damn pain would go away; the doc had dug the bullet out but Tyree could have sworn the pain was worse now than it had been at the time the thing had gone in.

'You in the mood for takin' some advice?' Tyree asked finally.

'No — but I figure you're going to hand some out anyway.'

Tyree sighed. Under normal circumstances Jim Travis was an approachable, easy-natured individual. It was said in Sweetwater that Jim Travis was the one man nobody could ever get mad at. Tyree reckoned he was getting close to changing that right there and then.

'Look, Jim, I know how you feel . . . '

'The hell you do!' Jim exploded. He snatched off his hat and slapped it against his leg in a moment of pure frustration.

Tyree watched him pace back and forth in front of the jail and decided to leave him to it. Let him work off some of that steam.

It was the best . . .

'Three thousand dollars!' Jim said suddenly. He spun on his heel and thrust out an arm, fingers stabbing in Tyree's direction. 'You know how long it's taken me to save that money, Sam?'

Tyree knew. Something like five years. Five long years of Jim Travis's life. Hard, back-breaking years. Herding cattle. Riding fence winter and summer. Trailing bawling herds across endless dusty miles to some distant market. Beneath a hot sun. Through rain and snow. Five years of that, plus taking on every extra chore that came along if it would add to his slowly mounting savings.

'Damnit, Sam, it's a hell of a piece of money to lose,' Jim said bitterly. He turned and stared across the street, narrowing his eyes against the hot glare of the sun slanting in over the rooftops. He was looking at the bank. Empty and deserted now, its big front window a black square, the big pane of ornately decorated glass shattered by a stray bullet during the robbery.

'You standing and staring at that bank ain't going to get it back, Jim.'

'I know that, Sam.' Jim moved and sat on the edge of the boardwalk. Again he glared at the lawman, and then just as quickly his lean brown face softened and he smiled. 'Hell, Sam, I'm sorry. You're the last one I should be taking it out on.'

'Makes you feel any better, you go right ahead,' Tyree said.

'Trouble is it doesn't,' Jim admitted.

Tyree glanced along the street. He watched a dark-suited figure approaching. 'Here comes an unhappy man.'

Jim raised his head and recognized Henry Sutton, the man who owned Sweetwater's bank.

'Sam,' Sutton said as he strode up to the boardwalk. He was a big man, running to fat. He always dressed well, exuding an aura of wealth and solidarity; now both the qualities seemed to have left him; he looked tired, confused, and Jim thought he looked frightened.

'What did the US Marshal's office have to say?' Tyree asked.

Sutton dragged a crumpled telegraph slip from his pocket. He held it up and shook it in Tyree's face. 'They sympathize but can't send us anyone down for at least a week. I ask you, Sam, what good is a week? Parsons and his bunch will have vanished long before that. So much for the law.'

Jim caught the hard expression that came into Tyree's eyes. For a moment he was sure Tyree was going to get up out of his seat. But the moment passed.

'So what do we do now?' Jim asked.

Sutton glanced at him as if he'd only

just become aware of Jim's presence. 'We?' he asked.

'Jim had three thousand dollars in your bank,' Tyree said quietly. 'Of course,' Sutton said. 'Well, my boy, the way things seem to be going at the moment I'm afraid your three thousand dollars looks like vanishing along with the rest of the bank's money.'

'You forget about it just like that?'

Sutton stared at him as if Jim had sprouted horns. 'What do you expect me to do?'

'Organize a posse or something to go after Parsons and his boys. Get the money back.'

'Are you serious?' Sutton smiled indulgently. 'Jesus, Sam, I do believe he is.'

Tyree studied Jim's face. 'Oh, he's serious, Henry.'

'I've never heard anything so ridiculous in my life,' Sutton said.

'Maybe you can afford to lose three thousand dollars,' Jim said. 'Mister, I can't. I've put too many years into getting that money. I don't intend

30

sitting round watching it vanish into thin air.'

'Travis, if you're so determined to get your money back I suggest *you* chase after the Parsons bunch and get it back.'

Tyree could have hit Sutton for saying that. He saw the stubborn gleam shine in Jim's eyes. The set of his jaw. The banker had said the wrong thing at the wrong time.

Without another word Jim turned away. He gathered the reins of his horse and climbed into the saddle. Easing the animal's head round he moved off up the street and out of town.

Tyree was in his office late that night. He had his seat in front of the pot-belly stove in a corner of the cluttered room. The glow from the stove was lulling Tyree to sleep as he sat there with a mug of hot coffee in his hands.

The door opened and Jim Travis stepped inside. He crossed to the stove and helped himself to a mug of coffee.

'Something you want?' Tyree asked.

'Tell me all you know about the Parsons bunch.'

'Damn me,' Tyree said. 'I knew it. You stubborn son of a bitch. Can't let it go, can you?'

'If you were me, Sam, would you let it go?'

The question silenced Tyree for a moment. He knew the answer only too well. 'They're a mean bunch, Jim.'

'I figured that much for myself.'

'I don't just mean hard men. Those fellers who ride with Parsons are the worst kind, Jim. They've killed a lot of people. Women as well as men. Life doesn't have much value for them. They'll kill a man soon as look at him. Last thing they ever think about is having a reason for killing a feller.'

'Sam, I'm nervous enough about this without you trying to scare me off. So quit it will you!'

Tyree swallowed the rest of his coffee. He stared at the glow of flame showing through the stove's half-open door. He could feel Jim's eyes on him and knew he was expected to offer some kind of help. Which made it all the harder. He liked Jim Travis, and it didn't sit easy being asked to advise on what might turn out to be downright dangerous.

'Look, Sam, I'm going whether you help me or not. It might be pure foolishness to everyone in this town, and I'm liable to get my head shot off doing it — but, Sam, I'd be a sight deader if I just sat back and forgot it. Three thousand dollars and five years is just too much to let go.'

'All right, Jim' Tyree said, knowing when he'd been outflanked. 'Sit down. It ain't a deal but I'll tell you what I know about Parsons and his bunch.'

The smell of brewing coffee brought Jim back to his lonely camp. He reached for the pot and lifted it from the fire, swearing softly as the hot handle seared his fingers. He wouldn't allow himself to put the pot down until he'd filled his tin mug; it was one of Jim's traits; a constant proving to himself of his own inner strength; a need for personal reassurance of his ability to survive in a hard and unrelenting world. Jim had been a survivor from an early age. Both his folks had died when he was five years old, and until he was old enough to earn his living, Jim had been passed back and forth between local families; there had been some good times, but in the main Jim had gone through a rough period. It had been a milestone in his life the day he'd signed on with a passing trail herd. From that day on Jim had become independent. He earned his keep and made it a rule never to become beholden to any man. He took to the miserable existence that was the lot of the drover as if he'd been born with a catch-rope between his teeth. After a few years drifting from outfit to outfit Jim had signed on with the AK crew, working for Al Keenan. The spread was situated a few miles from the town of Sweetwater. The job was as steady as any to be found in those days, and Jim had stayed . . .

Scooping crisp bacon from the pan Jim ate slowly, working out his plans for the following day. He hoped the rain held off. Once or twice he'd almost lost the fading trail; he needed all the luck he could get to stay with those tracks. A wry smile edged Jim's mouth — he needed a hell of a lot more than just luck! He finished eating, drained the pot of coffee, and cleared away his utensils. Before he turned in he checked that his horse was settled. Wrapping himself in his blanket Jim dragged his slicker over the top in case the rain did come during the night.

The morning he'd ridden out of Sweetwater there'd been a number of spectators, including Henry Sutton. Jim ignored the whole sorry bunch. As far as he was concerned they weren't there. He was still mad as hell with them after the way some of them had rounded on him in the saloon the night before. They'd gone and called him a trouble-maker. Making *them* look scared because *they* wouldn't do anything about going after Parsons and his bunch. *They* had families. Wives. Kids. Businesses to run. It wasn't their responsibility to go chasing outlaws all over creation. When Jim had pointed out that they'd had money taken too, well that had only got them even more worked up. The argument had got wilder. The accusations stronger. It had ended when Jim had stalked off out of the saloon, saying they could all go to hell, but *he* wasn't letting any damn outlaw ride off with his hard-earned cash, so he'd go and get it back by himself!

In the cold light of day the memory of his rash statement left Jim more than a little nervous. He was no lawman. No gunfighter. He'd never drawn his gun in anger against another human being. So what the hell was he doing getting set to chase off into the hills all by himself?

'Jim, you go careful now,' Tyree had said. He was standing on the edge of the boardwalk, outside the jail, Leaning heavily on a thick stick. 'Just remember what I told you about those fellers who ride with Parsons. Don't tangle with 'em 'less you have to. And if you get yourself in a corner don't stop to think about using your gun. Just use it, boy, and make damn sure you shoot straight.'

Settling in his cold saddle Jim had nodded to Tyree. He took up his reins. 'Thanks, Sam,' he'd said quietly.

Tyree had stared at him for a long moment, his eyes searching Jim's face. Then he inclined his head slightly. 'You'll do, boy.'

'See you, Sam,' Jim had said, touching his horse's sides. He'd ridden slowly out of Sweetwater, looking straight ahead, back rigid and wondering if he'd ever see the town again.

2

He was up and riding by the time daylight drove the shadows off the timbered slopes. Picking up the trail Jim followed it across high meadows and through a deep canyon that cut a ragged gash in the flank of the mountain. The canyon opened out onto a wide valley. On the far side of grass and timber Jim caught a glimpse of water sparkling in the crystal air. He drew rein and let his horse rest while he took in the scene before him. It was one of those awesome panoramas a man was apt to come upon in this unspoiled land; a vista of sheer beauty that took the breath away. He looked on the great tract of land, and he knew that somewhere he'd find a place like this and he'd take it for his own. It was his dream. The driving force that kept him going — that would *keep* him going until he got back the money he'd sweated for all those years.

Jim eased his horse down the long slope that would take him to the valley floor. He leaned back slightly in his saddle as the slope steepened. The warm sun burned through the back of his shirt. He caught the scent of pollen in the air. In the near distance he could even hear the heavy droning of a bee. It was that quiet. Almost as if he was the only human within a hundred miles.

The flat whip-crack report of a rifle going off told him he was wrong in thinking along those lines.

Jim *felt* the bullet pass him. It was that close. It was the first time he'd ever been shot at, but he reacted with an assurance that spoke more of pure desperation than practical experience. Jim let his boots slip from the stirrups, then left the back of his horse in an uncontrolled lunge towards the ground. He hit hard, the breath driven from his lungs, scrambling frantically for the closest cover — a low hummock yards to his left. Stumbling, sweat beading his face, he hurled himself behind the grassy mound a fraction of a second ahead of another shot that still tore a painful furrow across the top of his right shoulder. Jim slithered belly down, clawing his holstered Colt free.

The rattling echo of the rifle shots faded into silence. Jim hugged the ground, conscious of a nagging hurt where the bullet had gouged his shoulder; he could feel the sticky ooze of warm blood trickling down his back; a queasy sensation filled his stomach. Drawing himself close in to the base of the hummock he raised his head and peered across the tufted him.

He figured that the shots had come from the shadowed brush that flanked a stand of timber a couple of hundred yards across from him. Jim studied the area for a while; it *had* to be the place; there was no other cover close to. A movement off to his extreme left brought his head round with a snap; it was only his horse, moving restlessly.

Jim wished he was back in the saddle, digging in his heels and putting some distance between himself and the sneaky son of a bitch who'd tried to put a bullet in his back.

The gun in Jim's hand suddenly weighed heavy. He glanced down at it, the realization of what holding it implied — that he was thinking about taking another man's life. The thought scared him for a moment, but then he recalled Tyree's words. Sweetwater's lawman had been right. This was no game. It was deadly serious, and the man who didn't think straight was liable to end the loser. And in this kind of situation the loser didn't walk away when it was all over.

All right, you back-shooting bastard, let's see you try it when your target's facing you with a gun in *his* hand!

Jim had no intention of lying where he was for the rest of the day so he rolled away from the hummock, and dismissing the thought that he was probably doing a stupid thing, he came to his feet and ran directly for the brush in front of him. If he'd sat and thought about it he wouldn't have contemplated it, but he was good and mad, and that was as good an excuse as any.

He loosed off three spaced-out shots as he ran, changing his aim with each bullet, laying them along the span of the brush. As the third shot crashed out there was a noisy thrashing in the brush. As Jim twisted in that direction he caught a blurred glimpse of a dark figure bursting out of the brush; he had time for a quick impression of a bearded brown face, lips peeled back from large white teeth in a snarl of anger; there was a dark-blue shirt with a wide stain of red spreading across one side, just above the belt. He saw too the long rifle in the man's hands, sunlight glittering coldly on the steel barrel as the weapon was jerked into line with Jim's body. Jim went down on one knee, then forward, rolling desperately. Dimly he heard the heavy slam of the rifle as it fired. He felt dirt sting the side of his face as the bullet whacked the ground inches from him. Then he was throwing out his left hand to steady himself, his right bringing up the Colt in a smooth arc, finger surprisingly relaxed against the trigger. He held his aim for no more than a fraction of a second, then fired, dogged back the hammer and fired again. The blue-shirted man gave a hurt groan; his arms flew wide and skywards and he arched backwards, rising almost to the tips of his toes before toppling like a felled tree. His rifle flew from nerveless fingers, spinning over and over, catching the sun as it dropped to earth.

For a long time Jim stayed where he was. His eyes were fixed on the man he'd shot, almost as if he didn't accept what had actually happened. It seemed an eternity before he stood up, glancing around, then walked slowly to where the man was lying.

' . . . done for me, you son of a bitch,' the man was saying as Jim neared him; he was badly hurt yet his words came clearly and with considerable force.

'You didn't give me much choice,' Jim said. He became conscious of his gun, still dangling from his hand. He put it away as he knelt beside the man. He noticed there was a grubby bandage tied around the man's left thigh, the soiled cloth crusted with dark, dried blood. 'You catch that back in Sweetwater?'

The man grinned quickly, showing his large teeth. 'Damn lawman! Figured he was out of it, but the bastard still put one in me.'

Jim shoved his hat to the back of his head. He could hardly believe his luck. There he'd been thinking he was going to lose the Parsons bunch and now he had one of them right in front of him.

'Why'd they leave you behind?' he asked.

The man didn't answer for a while. He started coughing, pink froth bubbling from his lips. He drew in a few deep breaths. Then he stared at Jim, anger bright in his eyes.

'Ain't right for one man to catch all the bad luck,' he stated. 'I catch the damn bullet back in Sweetwater. Then those pissants leave me 'cause I can't stay in the saddle. Now you come along and shoot me to pieces. Jesus Christ, boy, life can be real miserable to a feller if she takes a mind.'

'Knew a preacher once who used to say every man sows his own seed an' collects the harvest.'

The man scowled darkly up at Jim. 'Meanin' what?'

'I guess it means you get what you deserve.'

'Boy, you're gettin' to be a pain in the ass! I had me a feelin' you'd be trouble soon as I spotted you trailin' us.'

'That why you took a shot at me?'

The man chuckled softly. 'Would have blowed you in half if I hadn't got the fever from that hole in my leg.' He spotted the blood staining the shoulder of Jim's shirt. 'Seems I clipped you anyways.'

'Why bother trying to stop me after

45

your partners rode off and left you?'

The man looked hurt. 'Hell, boy, they're my friends. Shit, you don't 'spect me to sit back an' allow you to ride on an' mebbe get the drop on 'em! What do you take me for?'

Confusion crowded Jim's mind. He couldn't understand the man's logic; later, though, thinking about it he did begin to see the man's reasoning; the rest of the bunch *were* his friends, probably the only true friends he'd ever had, and though they'd left him behind for their collective survival, he still felt obligated when they were threatened.

'You want to tell me where they're heading?' Jim asked.

'What do they call you?'

'Jim Travis.'

'I'll tell you something, Jim Travis. There ain't no way I'm going to tell you a damn thing. Now you save your breath an' let me die in peace. Least you can do for me seeing as you put me on the path.'

Jim walked away from the dying man,

knowing there wasn't a thing he could do. He collected his horse and led it to a tree, looping the reins. After a while he went back to where the man lay.

'Quit all that creeping around,' the man said. 'I ain't dead yet, Jim Travis, so just ease off.' He closed his eyes against a rise of pain, sweat glistening on his face. Then: 'Just why are you so eager to find Luke an' the boys?'

'I had money in the Sweetwater bank,' Jim told him. 'You took it and I want it back.'

'Hell, I didn't figure you for a rich man. How much we talkin' about?'

'Three thousand dollars.'

'You must miss that money awful bad to think about takin' on old Luke an' his boys.'

'Damn right I do,' Jim said.

The man didn't ask any more questions. When Jim took a close look he found the man was dead. He moved away and started to search for stones to cover the body. It took him a long time. Searching for a couple of lengths of timber Jim fashioned a rough cross and wedged it upright between a couple of flat rocks. It was all he could do for a man whose name he didn't even know.

Jim found the man's horse tethered in the trees. He unsaddled the animal and took off the bridle before he turned the beast loose. The horse wandered around for a while before it cut off across the slope and vanished from sight.

Jim climbed into his saddle and rode on. His shoulder was giving him a fair amount of pain but he wanted to get away from that hill and the mound of stones.

He kept riding until he reached the far end of the valley. Here he dismounted on the bank of the creek he'd first seen earlier. He took off his shirt and washed the wound in his shoulder. The cold water made the tender edges of the gouge tingle. Jim fished a clean kerchief out of his saddlebag and tied it clumsily across the top of his shoulder, bringing the ends under his arm. It wasn't the best bandage but it was going to have to do until something better came along.

Near the north end of the valley Jim picked up clear tracks; they showed that the bunch of riders were still making for the high country. Jim set his horse up the slope before him. As an afterthought he took out his rifle, checking that it was ready for use, and set it across the front of his saddle.

It started to rain about midafternoon. Jim had watched the big dark clouds scudding across the high peaks. He was almost able to predict the moment when the rain would start. As the first drops spattered his face Jim realized that he was going to be riding directly into the storm. He reached behind him and loosened his slicker. He drew it over his head, dragging the folds of water-proof material down to cover his body. He fastened the neck and jammed his hat back on seconds before the full force of the gathering storm barrelled down off the distant peaks

. . . heavy rain, driven by a rising wind, battered him. It stung his exposed face, ripping the breath from his throat. Jim lowered his head, narrowing his eyes while around him the grass and brush was mercilessly hammered by the elemental fury of the storm. The ground, previously hard-dry, swiftly became waterlogged. Overhead the sullen, dark-glowering clouds blotted out the blue of the sky. The light faded and the shadows lengthened.

Jim watched with dismay as the sluicing rain washed away the line of tracks he was following. He stared ahead, peering through the silver mist of rain. The rain couldn't last forever, he reasoned. And somewhere up ahead he could pick up those tracks again. One way or another he would . . . he had to . . .

3

He came on the small homestead in the final period of dusk. The light was slipping away quickly now. Already the high peaks were lost in a curtain of shadow and pouring rain. Jim might have ridden clear by the place if a lamp hadn't been lit inside the house, showing as a muted orange glow against the darker surroundings. He reined in his horse, gazing down the gentle slope beyond, eyes straining to make out the shape of the house and the outbuildings. He could make out the skeletal forms of corrals too.

Sitting there in the cold, with the rain dripping off the brim of his sodden hat, Jim debated whether to ride on or call at the house. His desire to make some kind of contact with the Parsons bunch was stifled by an admittance over the futility of riding on. It would be full dark soon and the storm showed no signs of slacking off; he wasn't going to achieve very much by wandering around the mountains all night; better to get a good night's rest, then move off at daylight. The thought of warm food and a dry place to sleep did a lot to persuade Jim to give up his pursuit of the Parsons bunch for the time being.

Jim cut down the slope and across the muddy yard in front of the house. He climbed stiffly down out of the saddle, his boots sinking into the soft earth. With his rifle in the crook of his arm he stepped to the door and knocked on the weathered panel. Nothing happened for a minute or so. Jim was about to knock again when he heard a bolt being drawn. The door eased open slightly, and then abruptly was thrown wide open.

Before Jim could react a dark figure appeared in the doorway, and the round black muzzles of a double-barrelled shotgun were jammed painfully against his chest.

'You just stand there, mister, and don't move until I tell you to!'

The voice was young and female — but that didn't lessen the potential danger of Jim's position.

'Look, I don't know what's got you all upset, but I ain't part of it.'

'How do *I* know that?'

'My name's Jim Travis. I've ridden up this damn mountain from a town called Sweetwater. About five days back Luke Parsons and his bunch robbed the bank and took every dollar in the place. Some of that money was mine and I want it back.'

The shotgun withdrew. The door was flooded with lamplight and Jim took his first look at the girl behind the shotgun.

'Come in out of the rain, Jim Travis, and welcome. I'm Jenny Mulchay.'

'My horse is . . .'

A slim hand reached out and drew him through the door. 'You look like a man who's ridden a long way. Get rid of that wet slicker and then take yourself over to the fire. There's a pot of coffee freshly made. Help yourself. I'll be back in a few minutes.'

'I can see to my own horse,' Jim protested. 'No call for you to get soaked.'

'You're a guest,' the girl said, her voice muffled by the folds of the heavy slicker she was donning. 'Besides this is a horse ranch, and I can find my round in the dark better than you could. So don't argue, Jim Travis.'

The door closed with a solid thump as she went out, leaving him alone.

Jim stood and took a long look around the big, low-ceilinged room. It was solid and comfortable, giving off an air of permanence. The warm air exuded mingled odours. The smell of tangy woodsmoke from the open hearth. The rich flavour of coffee. Jim thought he could smell meat roasting too and the warm smell of fresh-baked bread — unless his mind was in league with his stomach, playing tricks on him.

He became aware of rainwater dripping from his slicker onto the smooth-worn floorboards. He leaned his rifle against the wall and took the slicker off, hanging it on one of the pegs set into the wall beside the door. He dropped his hat over the top of the slicker, then turned and ventured deeper into the room. As he neared the fire, welcoming the heat that radiated from it, the aroma of hot coffee proved irresistible. The coffee pot, polished and gleaming, stood on a stone ledge at one side of the hearth. There was a china mug beside it and a small bowl of sugar. Jim poured himself a generous mugful, spooning in sugar. He took the drink and perched himself on the edge of a fat leather armchair.

The heat from the crackling fire lulled his senses. Overhead he could hear the steady drum of the rain on the roof. He drank the coffee, feeling it warm him deep down. He leaned back, allowing the heat from the fire to wash over him. The chair was so comfortable. It felt good. Really good . . .

Something snapped him out of it. Jim

sat up with a jerk, almost spilling the remains of the coffee out of the mug. His eyes focused on the shape kneeling before the fire.

'Steady there, Jim Travis, it's only me!'

Jim stared at the smiling girl. His first impression was of bright, penetrating eyes and a full, mobile mouth. A mass of dark hair curling around a face that was nothing less than beautiful.

'Sorry to be so rude, ma'am,' Jim apologized. He stood up, awkward in her presence, feeling as if he had taken advantage of her hospitality.

'Don't be silly,' she said, craning her neck to stare up at him. 'Now just you stand still long enough for me to say a few words.'

She rose to her feet and Jim was surprised to see how tall she was. Nor was she skinny, which almost always was the case with tall girls. She was wearing a much-washed check shirt and bleached Levis; shirt and pants had both been designed with men in mind and no accounting had been made for a full-breasted female with supple hips and long, trim legs.

'I've stabled and fed your horse,' Jenny said. 'I brought across your saddlebags and put them by the door. Are you hungry?'

'Yes, ma'am.'

He caught a defiant sparkle in her eyes — which he now saw were brown — and then she said firmly: 'It's Miss — not ma'am — but the name is Jenny.'

'Doesn't seem proper calling you by your first name . . . '

'While you're under this roof, Jim Travis, you'll oblige me by doing what I ask!'

'All right — Jenny.'

'Good. Now let's go and eat.'

On the far side of the room stood a heavy table, obviously made by some caring hands. Four chairs ringed the table.

'Sit down,' Jenny said.

Jim seated himself. An open doorway

led to a kitchen area built onto the rear of the main house. Jenny had vanished through the door and he could hear her moving around. Now he realized he hadn't been imagining the cooking meat. Jenny appeared shortly with a couple of plates and a large platter holding a joint of beef. She placed the things on the table and returned to the kitchen for dishes of browned potatoes and green vegetables. There was also a jug of rich gravy and a heaped plate of hot biscuits.

'Still hungry?' she asked as she sat down.

Jim found himself grinning. 'Yes.'

She carved him thick slices of beef, heaping on potatoes and greens. While she served herself Jim helped himself to gravy and biscuits.

'You say the Parsons gang robbed the Sweetwater bank?' Jenny asked after they had been eating for a while.

Jim nodded. 'Cleaned it out. Killed a man doing it and wounded the sheriff.'

'Sam Tyree?' Concern clouded Jenny's face. 'Is he badly hurt?'

'No. He took a bullet through the leg. He'll be on his feet again in a month or so.' Jim glanced up from his plate. 'You know Sam?'

'Yes. He's an old friend of my father.'

'Your father runs this place?' Jim asked. He'd been wondering about the ranch's men.

Jenny took a slow mouthful of food. 'He does when he's here,' she said.

Her tone caused Jim to stare at her. 'Where is he now?'

Jenny didn't answer immediately. She ran a trembling hand through her tangled hair.

'He in some kind of trouble?'

'I wish I knew,' Jenny said. 'He . . . he's out on that mountain somewhere. Chasing the Parsons gang.'

'They've been here?'

'Yes. They rode in two days ago and stole horses to replace theirs. Dad refused to just stand back and let them get away with it. He tried to stop them.

They just laughed at him and beat him until he couldn't stand. They could have killed him. After they'd gone I dragged him inside the house and got him cleaned up. I thought it was done with. But when I woke up the next morning Dad had gone. He left me a note telling me what he was doing. He told me not to worry. He said he just wanted his horses back.'

'I know how he feels,' Jim said. 'It's the same kind of feeling that brought me up here.'

Jenny's eyes blazed with frustrated anger. 'You men and your damned pride!'

'When it's all a man has he doesn't like losing it.'

'For half a dozen horses? For a handful of money?'

'The money's part of it, Jenny, but there's more to it,' Jim explained. 'For me it's five years out of my life. Five years of sweat and aching bones. Being frozen in winter and baked in summer. I reckon your father will be carrying the same notion.'

Jenny sighed. 'I can see there's no sense talking to you about it. You're on *his* side.'

After the meal they sat in front of the fire with fresh mugs of coffee.

'What are you saving the money for?' Jenny asked.

Jim smiled across at her. 'I want my own place. So I can be my own boss.'

'Cattle?'

'Horses,' Jim said. 'I've seen enough cattle.'

'You could do worse,' Jenny said. 'This is good horse country. Plenty of grass and water. Good protection from the bad weather.'

'I noticed while I was riding up.'

Jenny suddenly leaned forward to stare at his ripped shirt and the dark stains of dried blood. 'I didn't notice before. Are you hurt?'

'Just a scratch,' Jim said.

She moved to his side and ignoring his protests she opened his shirt to examine his shoulder.

'Heavens, that must hurt like mad.

Why didn't you tell me? Take off your shirt and I'll clean that wound out properly.'

'It'll be fine.'

'You take off that shirt, Jim Travis, and quit talking back. I'll stand no nonsense from you.'

While he took off his shirt Jenny brought warm water, bandages and ointment. It was as she was cleaning the raw, congealed gash that she asked the inevitable question.

'How did it happen, Jim?'

'I tangled with one of Parsons' men a ways back. They'd left him behind on account he was holding them up. Sam Tyree put a bullet in him back in Sweetwater.'

'And this man shot at *you*?'

'Yeah.'

'What happened, Jim?'

'We got it settled.'

Jenny turned to stare at him, her face set. 'You make it sound so final.'

'Killing a man is about as final as you can get.'

'But he *was* trying to kill you, Jim.'

'I guess so. It's what I keep telling myself.'

Jenny finished cleaning his shoulder. She put on some cooling ointment and then bandaged the wound.

'Do you have a clean shirt?'

'In my saddlebag.'

Jenny brought him the shirt and Jim put it on.

'Doesn't it make you want to quit? If you catch up to Parsons and try and get your money back it's bound to end in some kind of violence. Heavens, Jim, they outnumber you and they're men who live by the gun.'

'I know that.'

'Then how can you even . . . '

Jim grinned awkwardly, aware of the foolishness of his actions but still determined to follow them through.

'Jenny, it's the only way I can do it. I'll just have to face whatever it puts in my way.'

4

Five riders, hunched over in their saddles, black slickers glistening with rain. They held their mounts motionless beneath a curving overhang of crumbling rock, peering out from under the sodden brims of worn hats, eyes bleak in the gaunt planes of hungry faces. They watched in silence. Waiting. Affirming the uneasy feeling that had caused them to break their journey.

A distance away, moving slowly along a rain-misted ridge, came a lone rider. The man in the saddle held himself with extreme caution, head casting back and forth in anticipation of some unseen threat. He was following the five riders, and he had already gained enough knowledge about them to temper his thought of vengeance with restraint.

One of the five moved. Thrust aside

his cumbersome slicker with angry gestures. He leaned forward and slid his rifle from the sheath on the side of his saddle. Working the lever he put a cartridge in the breech. Then twisted his solid body round and brought the rifle to his shoulder. He let the distant rider reach a break in the ridge. The very place where he and his companions had reached the lower slope. When the rider was halfway down the loose, rain-washed slope, the rifleman touched the weapon's trigger. The rifle whacked out its brittle sound, the echo whipped away as swiftly as the wreath of powder-smoke by the drifting wind.

The rider sat sharp upright in his saddle and then rolled slowly off his startled horse. He struck the slope face down, arms and legs twisting loosely as he rolled over and over, coming to rest finally against a jutting rock.

The rifleman put away his weapon and pulled his slicker back into place. He sat watching the motionless figure splayed out on the distant slope.

65

'Stupid son of a bitch,' he said abruptly.

'Should have finished him back at that damn ranch.' The man who spoke cuffed back his shapeless hat, ignoring the chill rain that slapped at his unshaven face. 'Hell, he was stubborn enough then.'

'Well he's finished now, Nolan, so you can quit peein' your pants,' the first man said harshly. He was big and broad, and it showed despite the sagging folds of the wet slicker. Even his face was broad, the bones heavy, pronounced. He had penetrating, cold eyes shadowed by thick dark brows, and a wide nose. He wore a thick moustache on his upper lip, the ends curling down at the corners of his taut mouth. His name was Luke Parsons.

'You want to know something, Luke?' the man called Nolan said. He jabbed a thick finger at Parsons. 'This has been a horse-shit deal right from the start and it ain't gettin' no damn better.'

'What were you expecting? Goddam

66

roses and sweet music? I reckon you're gettin' old, Nolan. Maybe it's time we put you out to pasture.'

One of the other men laughed. 'Put him out to stud, Luke. Tether him in a field with half a dozen females and he can start siring his own little wild bunch.'

Nolan Troop scowled angrily. 'We going to ride? Or are you pissants figuring on sittin' out on this mountain permanent?'

Parsons pulled his horse's head round and dug in his heels, pushing the animal to a swift walk. He hunched his wide shoulders against the chill air, wishing they were over the mountains and down on the flat, sunbaked plain that would take them to the silent wilderness of the border country. He closed his ears to Nolan Troop's grumbling; though he would never have admitted it he sympathized with Troop; things hadn't gone too well for them from the moment they had ridden into Sweetwater; there was only one consolation — when life got as low as it was now it could only get better . . .

The tight group of riders faded into the grey mist of falling rain. After they had gone the only moving thing in the area was the horse of the man Luke Parsons had shot. It drifted back and forth across the distant slope, standing for long periods, head up as it search the surrounding terrain. Eventually it climbed back to the top of the slope and wandered into a nearby stand of timber.

After a long time the shot man moved. Slowly. Painfully. He raised his head from the saturated earth and stared about him. Time slid by with infinite deliberation. The man began to crawl up the slope. A foot at a time in the beginning. Then, as his strength slipped away, the feet became inches. Slow, tedious inches that sucked away the remaining energy. The man lay his face against the wet earth. He lay very still.

Towards dusk the rain slackened off and just before darkness fell it stopped altogether. The sun rose at dawn and flooded the land with brilliant light. By mid-morning the sun was high in a clear blue sky. A gentle breeze, warm and heavy with the scent of wild flowers, drifted down off the green slopes. It was almost as if the wild storm had never taken place. The sun dried out the land. It began to bake the earth hard once again. It dried the shallow claw marks the wounded man had gouged out of the mud. It crusted the earth clinging to his clothing and to his hands. The man himself moved for the first time since the sun had risen. He tried to raise himself but the effort proved too great. He only managed to start his wound bleeding again. He realized he was far too weak to help himself, and knew his only chance of survival lay in the hope of someone passing by who *might* spot him. He knew that possibility was slim, because this was lonely country, and few passed through.

So he lay, and he prayed that

someone would ride by. He drifted into unconsciousness again some while later, stretched out on that barren mountain slope.

And that was where Jim Travis found him.

5

Jenny had mentioned the existence of a neighbouring ranch further down the mountain and Jim figured he was closer to it than the Mulchay place. So he laid Jenny's father across his saddle, climbed back on his own horse and cut off across the sun-bright slopes.

Jim's knowledge of bullet wounds was basic. He'd seen one or two, but didn't have the experience to decide on the seriousness of Mulchay's wound. It was plain to see the man had lost a fair amount of blood. Yet he *was* breathing steadily. The one thing Jim did know for certain was that Jenny's father needed help, and he needed that help quickly.

It was the middle of the afternoon when Jim found Mulchay. He rode for close on two hours before he raised sight of the ranch; it was exactly as Jenny had described it — even down to the pleasant-faced woman scattering handfuls of corn for the chickens running free in the big yard fronting the house. As Jim rode in, skirting a big corral, the woman glanced his way. She stared for a moment, then stiffened. Placing her pail of corn on the ground she walked out to meet Jim as he reined in before the big house.

'That looks like John Mulchay,' she said. Her eyes searched Jim's face.

'It is, ma'am,' Jim said. He eased himself out of the saddle. 'He's hurt bad. Took a bullet and I reckon it's still inside.'

The woman nodded. She turned towards the house. 'Henry!'

Almost immediately a broad grey-haired man stepped out of the house. He took a quick look at the scene before him, then strode across the yard.

'It's John Mulchay,' the woman said. 'Been shot this young feller says.'

The man swung his head, scanning the seemingly empty yard. 'Buck! Charly! Get over here!'

Two men appeared from the far side of the yard, boots scuffing up the yellow dust.

'Give a hand, boy,' the grey-haired man said to Jim.

Between them they eased John Mulchay off the horse and into the arms of the two ranch hands.

'Take him inside, boys,' the woman directed. She took a quick look at the wound. 'I think we're going to need Doc Buford out here.'

Her husband nodded. 'Do what you can for him.' To Jim: 'You want to walk with me, boy?'

Jim fell in beside him. They crossed the dusty yard, heading for the big, sprawling stable on the far side.

'Tell me about it, boy.'

Jim told his story, from the time the Parsons bunch rode into Sweetwater and ending with his finding of John Mulchay.

'John is a good friend. I'm obliged for what you've done, Jim.' The man held out a big, work-roughened hand. 'I'm Henry Treece.'

They entered the stable. Horses stirred restlessly, stamping against the hard-packed floor. Dust motes drifted lazily in thin shafts of sunlight.

'Tom!'

A bow-legged figure eased out of the shadows. Bright eyes glittered fiercely from a seamed, brown face that held a lifetime of experience.

'Put a saddle on a fast horse, Tom, and get over to Ellington. Find Doc Buford and get him back here. Tell him John Mulchay's bad hurt and needs him.'

The man called Tom turned without a word and vanished into the depths of the stable.

Henry Treece led Jim back to the house. They entered the wide, low-ceilinged living-room and Treece motioned for Jim to sit down.

'Coffee?'

Jim nodded. He perched himself on the edge of a big leather armchair and gazed around the room. He was impressed. Treece was obviously a man who had worked hard. Built his place with pride. It showed in the room and the furnishings.

'Here,' Henry Treece said. He had returned from the kitchen with mugs of hot black coffee.

'Thank you, sir.'

Treece sat himself in a chair across from Jim, watching the younger man, 'So you intend to settle with Luke Parsons and his bunch all by yourself?'

'I don't expect it to be easy,' Jim answered.

Treece chuckled softly. 'Damned if you ain't got the gall to just do it,' he said. 'But you've set yourself one hell of job.'

'So everybody keeps telling me.'

'But you just keep on going all the same.'

'In my place what would you do?'

Treece sat back, a distant expression clouding his eyes for a moment. 'If I was thirty years younger and I'd lost what you have, why I reckon I'd be chasin' Luke Parsons too.'

Jim nodded. 'Chasing 'em seems to be all I'm doing. I lost their trail back a ways. During that storm.'

A thoughtful look crossed Treece's face. He stood up and crossed the room. Going to a roll top desk he opened a drawer and took out a rolled map which he spread out on a nearby table.

'Take a look here,' he said.

When Jim had joined him Treece pointed out positions on the map.

'We're here. You found John somewhere here? From what I know of Parsons he'll be heading for the border. Seems he has friends in Mexico. I've heard tell he holes up in a town called Valerio. There.'

Jim studied the map, memorizing the winding trail he was going to have to follow. Down the mountain slopes and onto the shimmering flatland that stretched wide and empty all the way to the border.

'Between here and the border there are a few hard places, Jim. Near desert.

Short on water and long on hot, dry days. Ain't much lives out there 'cept rattlers — some with two legs, and a few Apaches. Now I ain't one for butting in on a man's business, Jim, and you tell me if I go too far. But it could be damn hard on you down there. You won't find many friends. In fact I'd keep my eye on anybody you meet. Parsons has a few friends and they tend to gather in that border country. It's handy for them to jump over if things get too hot.'

'I appreciate your advice, Mister Treece, and I don't want you to think I'm not grateful.'

Treece held up a hand. 'But you're still going — I know.'

'Not before he has a good meal inside him.'

Jim and Henry Treece turned to see Mrs Treece standing in the kitchen doorway.

'I'm not sure what foolishness you're up to, Jim Travis, and I don't think I want to. That can wait until you've eaten and had a good night's sleep. And I want no arguments.'

'Ma'am, I wouldn't dream of arguing.'

* * *

He took his leave of the Treece place the next morning. Henry Treece followed Jim outside to where his horse was waiting. The animal had been fed and watered. Jim's saddlebags were stuffed with food from Mrs Treece's kitchen and there was an extra canteen of water hanging on his saddle.

'Will you see to it that Jenny gets to know about her father?' Jim asked.

Henry Treece nodded. 'Don't worry about Jenny. We'll see she's looked after.' Treece smiled slowly. 'I'd say you've taken a shine to that girl.'

Jim concentrated on fixing his saddlebags in place. Finally he said: 'I aim to call on her when this is over.'

'Knowing Jenny I'd say you'll be more than welcome, boy.'

Jim swung into his saddle and took up the reins. 'Thanks for everything, Mister Treece.'

'You're purely welcome, Jim. Take care now and remember you have friends here.'

6

Jim picked up the trail again on the third day out from the Treece place. Tracks left by five horses heading south, and no more than a day — maybe a day and a half — old. He figured that by now the Parsons bunch would be feeling pretty safe; apart from John Mulchay there hadn't been any pursuit, so they would be congratulating themselves on getting away with the Sweetwater raid; their confidence would relax them, decide on them slowing their pace.

It was a good time for him to make a try at getting his money back, Jim decided. While the Parsons bunch were beginning to ease their guard. He didn't fool himself into believing there wouldn't be any risks at all. Anything he did that concerned the Parsons bunch would be dangerous by definition. Off guard or not they were still professional gunmen. Killers. The type who shot first and never even thought about wondering why. So however he approached the problem he had to keep in mind the possibility of finding himself on the hard end of someone else's bullet. It was a less than comforting thought.

An hour after noon Jim stopped to give his horse a rest. He reined in beside a narrow stream that came winding down out of the high hills behind him. Letting his horse drink Jim knelt beside the stream and sluiced the clear, cool water onto his face, feeling it rinse away the gritty dust clinging to his stubbled flesh. Rising to his feet he wandered to the crest of a low rise and stared out across a wild and seemingly endless tract of semi-arid land. It lay dun-coloured and shimmering beneath a burnished curve of blue sky that was marred only by a few thin scraps of white cloud. Henry Treece had been right. It was rough country. Jim sank down on his heels, resting his arms across his knees. He gazed southwards, shading his eyes against the harsh brightness of the sun. After some time he reached up and took off his hat, drawing his free hand through his hair. *Hell, Jim boy, maybe you've bit off more'n you can handle!* The thought drifted into his mind unbidden, and the simple act of even admitting the possibility he might be taking on overwhelming odds made him angry. It was akin to accepting failure, which was something Jim Travis never could.

He rose to his feet and stalked grimly back to his horse. Gathering the reins he swung into the saddle, setting the horse into motion with an angry jab of his heels. He rode away from the stream and crossed the final slope of the foothills to reach the silent wilderness of the flatlands.

Jim rode hard for the rest of the afternoon. An hour before dark he reined in as his aching eyes picked out the irregular shape of what could have only been a town some miles ahead. He sat for a while, staring at the dusty outline, and eventually moved off again. There was no doubt in his mind that the tracks he was following were aiming directly for the town.

He rode in after dark, passing the skeletal outlines of cattle pens and loading platforms that lay alongside a single-span railroad track. Just beyond the tracks lay a huddle of crude adobe huts and Jim caught the smell of spiced food cooking, heard the soft accents of Mexico. The way led him up a rutted slope that opened onto the town's main street. He rode by stores that were still open for business and saloons that were *just* opening for the night ahead.

Jim spotted a hotel and took his horse over to the hitch rail. He climbed down, took his rifle and saddlebags and went inside. The lobby was dim, the air warm and smelling of dust. Jim's boots rapped against the worn floor as he crossed to the desk where a middle-aged man watched him with total disinterest.

'Single room,' he said. 'Just for the night.'

The clerk reached behind him and hooked a key off the board. He dropped it in front of Jim. 'Sign the book. Room'll be two dollars. Pay me now.'

Jim signed the yellowed page of the register. He fished out a couple of silver dollars and shoved them across the desk.

'Where can I get a meal?'

'Out the door. Turn left. There's a place a few doors down.'

Jim took his key and climbed the creaking stairs. His room turned out to be on the front, overlooking the street. He tossed his gear on the bed and opened the window.

'Where are you, boys?' he asked softly, staring out of the window, and along the street. He knew damn well that he could be too late. The Parsons bunch had ridden into this town — it was entirely possible that they had already ridden out again.

Jim cleaned himself up as best he

could, put on his last clean shirt and left the hotel. He found the place the clerk had mentioned. It was a small, but pleasant restaurant run by a dark Italian and his wife. They provided plain food that was at least well cooked. Jim had a steak with potatoes and greens, followed it with some stewed apples and a pot of rich coffee. He lingered over the meal, giving the saloons time to fill before he started visiting them. If Parsons and his bunch had spent any time in this town the saloons were the likely places for picking up any information. It was also a risky way of doing it but Jim had no other options.

It turned out to be a long and fruitless night. Jim moved from saloon to saloon, even chanced a visit to the two cantinas down in the Mexican section of town. He didn't learn a thing apart from confirming his own suspicions that he was no drinking man. Somewhere close on midnight he made his way back to the hotel. He had spent too much of his money, swallowed too much bad liquor, and his only gain was a hell of a headache. He wasn't exactly drunk but his senses were dulled enough so that he didn't even see the two dark figures closing in on him until it was too late. Far too late.

Jim's first warning of trouble came in the form of a hard fist slamming into his left side. The blow drove the breath from his body, pain flaring up through his ribs. And then a hard bulk smashed against him, driving him sideways into the dark mouth of an alley. He tried to keep his balance, but hard punches came at him from the shadows, bouncing him against the rough planks of a building. The back of his head crashed against the planking. A savage blow numbed his jaw, filling his mouth with the taste of blood. Jim struck out wildly, felt his fist connect with soft flesh. Dimly he heard a man curse. And then the beating began again. They knocked him to the ground, dragged him up again, kicking and punching until he was so much dead weight in their arms.

A hand took hold of his hair, dragging his head back. Jim coughed up blood from his throat and spat it out. A man laughed. Close by a match flared and Jim blinked at the sudden bright light.

'You hear me, boy?'

Jim croaked his answer.

'Word is you've been all over town tonight askin' questions. Now I'm askin' one. What's your business with Luke Parsons and his boys?'

'My business,' Jim husked, forcing the words from his swollen throat.

'Looks like we got us a hard one, Will,' the second man said.

'They can die just like anyone else.'

The match held near Jim's face went out. The man cursed. There was a pause as he fumbled for another, scraped it alight. This time Jim caught a glimpse of the face behind the ring of flame. He made a mental note of a thick, hooked nose and narrow grey eyes.

'You think of a right answer, boy, 'cause I don't like a smartmouth. Just what is it you're after?'

Jim's bottled-up frustrations boiled to the surface in a rush and he struggled against the hands holding him down.

'Damnit, he's got something that belongs to me and I aim to get it back!'

The man called Will chuckled. 'Hell, boy, if everybody Luke Parsons has stole from come after him this town'd have half the territory in it!'

'I don't reckon we'll have much trouble with this one,' the second man chuckled. 'He ain't but a kid.'

'Tell you something, boy,' Will said. 'You're lucky it was only me and Lee you crossed. Luck too that the others already rode on. If you'd bumped into Nolan Troop or Luke himself . . . well, hell, boy, you'd be dead right now!'

'That supposed to satisfy me?'

Will grunted in annoyance. 'Boy, you're startin' to rile me. I'll give you some advice. I were you I'd get me on a horse and go home. Whatever it is you lost it ain't worth the dyin' for.'

The one called Lee jerked brutally against Jim's hair. 'You hear him? Hear him good, boy, 'cause if I set eyes on you again I won't come at you with words.'

'That's a promise,' Will agreed. 'Show your face in town come daylight you'd better do it with a gun in your hand!'

The match was snuffed out. Darkness rolled over Jim as he slid to the ground, his face pressed against the dirt. He heard the faint scrape of boots against the ground, the muted jingle of a spur, and then it all melted away. It became very quiet. He lay and decided it was in his best interests to stay where he was for a while. He was starting to hurt . . .

7

The pain was still there but the flood of wild, unreasoning rage had practically blotted it out. Hurt as he was, his body pulsing fiercely with every step he took, Jim walked out of the dark alley and along the deserted street. His good sense told him he was acting like a fool kid, allowing his temper to get the better of him — yet he knew, deep down, that come hell or high water, he was going to find the two men responsible for his condition and square the account. There was no way he could ride out of town just because they'd told him to. It was pride bordering on vanity almost, but it meant the difference between walking upright on two legs or crawling in the dirt like a whipped dog.

Along the street, where lamplight threw yellow pools into the darkness, he could hear noise and laughter. In the background the tinny sound of a piano. As he neared the source, a smoke-filled saloon, the batwing doors swung open and an unsteady figure swayed out onto the scuffed boardwalk. Jim had one foot on the step as the man leaned out to grasp the porch support, resting his weight against the weathered timber. Their eyes met for a brief instant.

'Looks like it's been a rough night for the both of us,' the man mumbled, staring at Jim's bloody face.

'Yeah — but yours is over,' Jim said and moved on by.

He stood at the door, peering into the saloon. A feeling of utter frustration swept over him as he scanned the crowded interior.

Dammit, where were they? He sighed wearily, admitting that he was clutching at straws. There was no way of knowing where those two had gone. No reason to think they were here in *this* saloon. They could have gone anywhere in town.

Jim had already started to move back from the door when he caught a glimpse of a vaguely familiar face. He focused his attention on the man who was sitting at a table on the far side of the saloon. Jim stared long and hard. There was a second man at the table, his back to Jim. The one facing in Jim's direction leaned forward, catching the full glare from one of the lamps suspended from the ceiling.

It was the hard-faced man from the alley! The one who had spoken to Jim. The one who had warned him off. He felt his blood rise. Became aware of the wildness boiling over, urging him to . . .

Jim was inside the saloon without being aware of having moved. Oddly, above the general din, he could hear the batwing doors creak behind him as they swung on dry hinges. Jim made his way across the saloon, ignoring the curious stares. He threaded his way in and out of the crowded tables. Men still looked at him, eyeing the bruised and bloody face, the dirt-streaked clothing. Yet there was something in Jim's expression that made them step aside.

And then the man called Will spotted him. His heavy features darkened in a scowl. A forewarning of Jim's intentions promoted him into startling movement. Yelling a warning to his partner Will rolled sideways out of his chair, twisting his body as he hit the floor so that when he rose to his feet he was facing Jim, his gun up and firing.

Knowing he had only seconds, Jim launched himself forward in a long dive that took him to the floor. While he was falling his fingers were plucking his gun from its holster, thumb rolling back the hammer. He broke his fall with his left hand, the impact jarring his shoulder, snatching the breath from his lungs. He heard the loud slam of a gunshot and felt something tug at his shirtsleeve. He pushed his gunhand forward, tilting the muzzle of the weapon up, aiming between the curved backs of suddenly vacant chairs. For a fraction of a second the man named Will appeared to be frozen in Jim's sights and he triggered a frantic shot. Gathering his long legs beneath him he thrust up off the floor. As he uncoiled his lean body a gun exploded close by and a hungry pain filled his right side. He stumbled, off balance, catching his hip against a table. Another shot rang out, exploding needle-sharp splinters of wood from the table top into the side of his face. Jim dragged his gunhand round to the right, triggering as he saw the rising bulk of a man's body. Saw the dull gleam of a smoking gun in a clenched fist. His bullet hit high in the chest, throwing the man back, arms wide apart.

'Damn you . . . ' Will yelled.

Jim spun on his heel at the cry, his gun following in a reflex movement. He saw the man named Will, only yards away. Crouching, his face twisted with rage. Will's gun was pointing at Jim and the hammer was already dropping as Jim fired himself.

The two shots were close enough to sound as one.

Something ripped through Jim's left arm, high up. The impact twisted him round. He fell, pain sickening him. He slumped against the floor, putting his weight on one arm and was surprised to see bright splashes of blood on the scuffed floorboards.

Get up! On your feet dammit! Get up 'cause they ain't going to wait! Jim's mind screamed the command to a body unable to respond. He could hear a rising roar of sound — voices mingling until they were a blur — and above it all lay a pulsing throb that rose and overwhelmed him completely.

8

Brilliant, hurting sunlight stung his eyes. Jim turned his head to one side, awareness of where he was dawning swiftly. A quiet, pleasant room. He was lying flat on his back in a soft bed with clean white sheets. In the background muted sounds. A closer sound drew his attention.

'Hurts I dare say.'

'Some,' Jim answered. He could feel a dull, deep-down ache in his side; a raw, nagging pain like an exposed nerve in a bad tooth. 'No, damn, it hurts a lot!'

'Body goes round getting in the way of bullets then I reckon he deserves to hurt.'

The speaker moved into Jim's vision, eyeing him with the intensity of a vulture sizing up a potential victim. Jim saw a grey-haired man dressed in a crumpled black suit. A craggy brown face with a lot of wry humour behind the gruff exterior.

'They call me Quincey. Doc Quincey. Tell me something, boy, you got something against growing old?'

Jim frowned at the unexpected question. 'Not sure what you mean, Doc.'

'I mean going up against Will Loomis and Lee Brown. Boy, that was a damn fool thing to do.'

'Wasn't exactly the way I had it planned. Not a shootout.'

'Whatever, just tell me why.'

'I had my reasons.'

Quincey shook his head. 'They to do with that beating somebody gave you?'

'Maybe.'

'Boy, you're one hell of a conversationlist.'

'Doc, what happened to Loomis and Brown?'

'Some gunfighter you are,' Quincey sighed. 'Loomis is dead. Brown's recovering from the bullet you put in him and waiting for the US Marshal to collect him. I hear you'll be picking up some reward money on those two.'

'I don't want any reward money,' Jim said defensively.

'And there I was thinking I might get paid for a change!'

'You'll get paid, Doc.'

Quincey sat on the edge of the bed. He took off his steelrimmed spectacles and began to wipe them with a crumpled handkerchief.

'You did a fair amount of talking while you were getting over that fever.'

'What fever?'

This time Quincey smiled. 'You wouldn't know about that. Almost four days since they brought you here. I had to leave my bed to cut out that bullet. You were lucky. It bounced off a rib. If it hadn't you'd be watching the grass grow from the root end. But I reckon you'll mend.'

'I'm obliged for what you did, Doc. How long before I can get up?'

'There you go again! All set to go

chasin' off 'fore you're ready.'

'I've got things to do that won't wait.'

Quincey poked a long finger at Jim's chest. 'Like finding Luke Parsons?'

'Maybe.'

'Maybe nothing, boy. Like I said you did a fair piece of talking under that fever, and I'm a good listener.'

'I'd say you got a bad habit there, Doc.'

'Well I've stayed healthy for a lot of years and I'm too damn old to change my ways now.' Quincey stroked his stubbled chin. 'You want tell me if I heard everything right?'

Jim smiled. 'I guess I owe you that much.'

'What's so important it makes you want to brace Luke Parsons?'

'Parsons and his boys raided the bank back in Sweetwater. Took every penny in the place. Including what I had there.'

'Hard-earned?'

'Doc, I'm just a working hand. Took me a long time and a lot of sweat to build my stake. I want it back.'

'How much?'

'Three thousand.'

Quincey nodded. 'Appreciate how you must feel. That's a fair piece of money in any man's language.'

'So when can I ride, Doc?'

'If I told you to rest for four or five days you wouldn't listen.'

'Damn right I wouldn't.'

'Don't come back complaining if you fall off your fool horse.'

'Don't worry about me, Doc.'

Quincey cleared his throat. 'Ain't likely to, boy,' he said without too much conviction.

The marshal arrived on the evening train. His name was Beckmann. A tall, spare man with greying hair and eyes like cold flint. He made his feelings clear to Jim within minutes of speaking to him.

'Boy, if you weren't in that bed I'd be kicking your ass clear out of town. What is it? You tired of living?'

'Marshal, all I want is my money

back. The way I see it if I don't go after Parsons nobody else will.'

'Tyree said you were a stubborn son of a bitch. He was right. Damnit, boy, is it really worth it? For three thousand dollars? Money won't be much use when you're buried.'

'You expect me to ride back to Sweetwater? Just forget about my stake and go on being a forty-a-month-and-found ranch hand for the rest of my life! If that's what I'm expected to do, Marshal, I might as well *be* dead!'

Beckmann made an angry sound. He stared around the room as if he was looking for something to hit.

'It ain't likely to get any easier, boy,' he said finally. 'Luke Parsons doesn't stay on this side of the border any longer than he has to. He isn't like his boys. He puts off playing around until he's safe in Mexico. That's where he'll be now. Where the law can't touch him.'

'You forget, Marshal. I'm not the law,' Jim said. '*I* can touch him.'

Beckmann sighed. 'I was afraid you'd

say that. You think on, boy. It's right when you say you can go where the law can't — but it's also right that once you cross over that border the law can't help you either. You'll be a damn sight more on your own than you are now.'

'That won't be new to me, Marshal,' Jim said. 'I've been looking after myself since I could walk.'

'Boy, you're hard as a whore's heart. Mind you'll need to be if you're aimin' to call out Luke Parsons in his own backyard.'

'I can't see him giving up my money if I send him a damn letter.'

A smile edged Beckmann's lips. 'Time was when *I* felt the way you do,' he said. 'Ten feet tall and so damn sure I could take on the whole world. That's one of the troubles with getting older. You start to see you aren't as smart as you thought you were. Or as tough.'

'Trying to tell me I should quit while I'm ahead, Marshal?'

The marshal shook his head. 'You know your own mind, boy, and you're of an age to run your own life. Just make sure you're certain that what you go after is worth the risk.'

★   ★   ★

Sleep was a long time coming to Jim that night. He lay staring up at the ceiling, not really seeing the slanting shadows etched across the plaster. His mind was crowded with conflicting thoughts.

On one level was the debate over whether he *was* doing the right thing. Risking his life because of a sum of money. Giving up would have been easy right there and then. No one could have accused him of quitting. Not after all he'd been through. He could ride back to Sweetwater safe in the knowledge that he had at least tried. Yet going back empty-handed would also be an admission of failure. Not that he had anything to prove to anyone but himself. The fact of giving up would be something he would carry himself. He

103

would have to live with it. But it was something he *wouldn't* live with. If he could quit now he could do the same every time life became difficult. It wasn't a prospect that sat easy on his conscience.

Strangely he experienced less of a problem with the aftermath of the gunfight with Loomis and Brown. He had been forced into a killing situation and had reacted from a desire to survive. Only now could he sit back and question his motives in going into that saloon.

True he had wanted a squaring of accounts with the two outlaws. But not to the extent of having to kill. Or had he? Perhaps he had been hoping they might push things to a point where the use of guns became unavoidable. It made little difference now. The decision had been taken from him the moment Will Loomis had seen him. From that instant the gun had become the deciding factor, and no amount of not wanting it would have changed things.

Loomis had laid down the ground rules — fight or die — and Jim had responded.

Whatever else he might waver on there remained a constant determination in his mind. He still needed to find Luke Parsons. Nothing would deter him from that.

9

'Well?'

Nolan Troop didn't answer straight off. He walked back to his horse and eased himself into the saddle. There was a hard set to his jaw and a distant gleam in his eyes. Luke Parsons had seen that expression before. From past experience he knew it spelled trouble.

'*Nolan?*' Parsons put a deliberate emphasis on the word. Troop responded slowly. He jabbed a finger in the direction of the village below them. 'Something ain't right, Luke,' he said.

'Why? What did you see?'

'Nothin'. It's all pretty as you please. Just like it always is.'

Parsons glanced beyond Troop to where the third member of the group sat silent and motionless on his horse. 'Fargo?'

'Like Nolan says — she looks fine. I

reckon that'll do for me.'

'I only *said* it looks fine,' Troop snapped. 'I also said something ain't right.'

'But you haven't said what.'

'Come on, Luke, you've had feelings about something being wrong yourself. Ain't something you can point at 'cause it's inside. A gut feeling.'

Fargo hawked noisily and spat. He wiped his sleeve across his mouth. 'My gut's telling me I ain't had a half-way decent meal in a long time. Sittin' up here ain't about to remedy that condition. So let's quit actin' like a bunch of old ladies an' get on down there.'

'Got to admit he's talking sense, Nolan,' Parsons said. 'We've come a hell of a way.'

Troop scratched his unshaven jaw. He raised his shoulders in a gesture of defeat. He dug in his heels and took his horse out from the shade of the thick stand of brush and onto the dusty slope that led to the village. Parsons and

Fargo trailed behind him, letting their tired horses pick a slow gait. Fine dust rose from beneath the plodding hooves, hanging in the dry, hot air.

As they neared the village, Troop reached down and took out his rifle. He worked a shell into the breech and laid the weapon across his thighs. After a moment Fargo did the same. So did Parsons. It was a purely defensive measure. They were all men who lived on their wits and their ability to foresee possible trouble.

Valerio was one of those ancient Mexican settlements that gave the impression it had been there right from the day of Creation. An untidy tangle of stone and adobe. Crumbling old houses. A church with a high tower holding a big bell. Some buildings gleamed with coats of thick whitewash. Others had faded to a pale, bleached shade that blended in with the dust continually blowing in and out of the crooked streets and narrow alleys. The pace of life in Valerio was measured and even. Nothing was allowed to disturb the established routine of life. Not that the inhabitants of Valerio were passive observers. They were aware of the way of the world. That they lived in hard and often violent times, and that *meant* an opportunity was to be grasped and made to profit. It was the only reason why Parsons and his men were made welcome in the village. The *gringos* brought money to Valerio. So they were tolerated. And that tolerance would last just as long as it was profitable.

'Damn place is quiet as the grave,' Parsons muttered sourly as the three neared the outskirts of the village. He was beginning to experience the same feeling Troop had. *Shit, I should have listened to Nolan*, he thought.

'Something stinks,' Troop said forcibly. 'I knew it. Goddam it to hell!'

Parsons abruptly yanked back on the reins, causing his horse to falter.

'Luke?' Troop's query was brittle.

'On the roof. The *cantina*. I seen him. Son of a bitch moved.'

'*Who?*'

'*Rurales!* Ain't no way I'd mistake those boys.' Troop was already scanning the terrain surrounding them, seeking a way out. He knew their time was short. Once the waiting Mexicans realized they had been seen they would come boiling out of the village with guns blazing.

'We head east,' he said. 'Into the lava-beds. It's the only chance we'll have of losing them. If we can give them the slip we can cut off to the north.

'That'll take us back over the border,' Fargo protested.

'If we've got the *Rurales* on our trails there ain't going to be any place in Mexico *I* want to be,' Troop said angrily.

'Me neither,' Parsons agreed. 'Let's get the hell out of here.'

They drove their horses into motion as one, setting the startled animals to running. Almost in the same instant came a distant shout from the direction of the village. A ragged volley of shots crackled through the air, but the distance was too great for sustained accuracy. They knew, though, that it was a condition capable of being remedied by the *Rurales* once they took up the pursuit. Which they would. The Mexican law force, despite the rumours about its capabilities, had a reputation for dogged persistence when it came to staying with its quarry. They also had the advantage of being in their own territory. No one knew it better. Or used it to the best advantage.

They rode hard, knowing that their horses were already tired and couldn't be expected to maintain the kind of pace now expected from them. But there was no alternative. It boiled down to a simple choice. Make a stand — and die. Or run — and hope to elude the *Rurales*. The risk of death lay with both choices. It could come during a fight or after capture by the *Rurales*. A quick end would be favoured. The justice of the *Rurales* could be, and often was, crude and violent. It was not the way any man would choose for himself. Even if he was granted the luxury of choice.

To the east of Valerio the land fell away in a series of long slopes dotted with shallow gullies and patches of thick, tangled brush. Beyond lay the lava-beds. A vast tract of twisted and tortured black rock thrown up during some prehistoric period; molten rock that had cooled into solid material that had been shaped and worn by the elements. It was an inhospitable place. Virtually devoid of vegetation. Bone dry and scoured by drifting sand and dust. Its only saving grace lay in its mazelike formation of natural tunnels and crevices. The formless jumble of shattered, broken heaps of rock provided ideal places of concealment. There were no trails to follow. No worn paths.

Nolan Troop was the first to reach the fringes of the lava-beds. He drew rein and turned in his saddle to cast a sharp eye along their backtrail.

'They showing yet?' Parsons asked. He pulled his lathered horse alongside Troop's.

'Damn right they are,' Troop replied bitterly.

They watched the drifting dust staining the horizon. Moments later they were able to see the group of riders themselves.

'Some peace we're going to get,' Troop muttered darkly.

Parsons shrugged. 'Valerio always did right for us before.'

'Yeah? Well that's going to comfort me no end,' Troop told him.

'What the hell do you want me to do? Apologize?'

Troop swore angrily. He yanked his horse's head round and took the animal across the hard black rock, heading for the rising mass of the beds. Fargo followed close, leaving Parsons to bring up the rear. They were forced to walk the horses. The surface of the rock underfoot was hard and glass-smooth in places. The nervous horses took a dislike to the slippery surface, and they started to play up.

'Hold still you son of a bitch!'

Fargo's outburst only served to startle his skittish mount. It snatched its head away from his tight rein, kicking out and then panicking as it lost its grip on the rock. Fargo hauled up on the reins, making a desperate attempt at keeping the animal on its feet. He realized the futility of the effort, dragging his feet clear of the stirrups as the horse went over. Its shrill scream of fright mingled with Fargo's wild curses as he hit the hard rock and slithered helplessly down a steep drop.

'Shit!' Parsons yelled. He dropped from his own saddle, hanging on to his reins as he peered over the edge of the drop. He could see Fargo thrashing his way out of a tangle of thornbush. 'You all right?'

'Sure,' Fargo said. 'I'm down here 'cause I like the goddam view.'

'Get your ass back up here,' Troop told him. 'I don't fancy hanging around too long with those greasers close enough to . . . '

The whack of a rifle firing was followed by the whine of the bullet bouncing off rock. It struck yards to Parsons' left.

Troop turned in his saddle, rifle sweeping round in a glittering arc. His eye had spotted the target long before his weapon's muzzle was lined up. He touched the trigger. Smoke lanced from the muzzle, the sound of the shot echoing through the rocks.

'Nolan?' Parsons asked.

'Got the bastard.'

The sound of the shots had a telling effect on Fargo. He scrambled up the steep slope and ran to his horse. The animal had regained its feet and was standing in a passive, head down pose. Fargo snatched up the dangling reins, raining curses on the unfortunate animal.

'Let's go! Let's get the hell under cover!' Troop's voice whiplashed across the beds.

They dragged their weary horses behind them, aware that at any moment a hail of bullets could come at them.

The first shots that did come were still off-target. The next volley brought a number of near-misses. Chips of black rock were gouged from the surface. Sharp splinters peppered Troop's face as one bullet howled off the side of a shoulder-high boulder he was passing. The pain brought a characteristic response. Troop spun on his heel and pumped a half-dozen shots in the general direction of the advancing *Rurales*.

Fargo, impatient with the slow progress, jammed his rifle back in its scabbard and dragged himself back into his saddle.

'The hell with this,' he roared. 'I'm movin' on.'

'Fargo! Get off that damn horse!'

Parsons' yell was swamped by the rattle of shots. Fargo rose in his stirrups, arms thrown forward. The right side of his shirt burst open in a ragged spray of red. He cried out once.

Then he keeled over and fell from the back of his horse. He hit the hard rock on one shoulder, turning over a couple of times before coming to rest at the base of a high rock. He arched his body and made an uncoordinated attempt at standing up. Blood was trailing from the gaping tear in his shirt. The left side of his face had been scraped raw where he'd hit the rock. He got one leg under him and hunched himself up the side of the rock. He clamped his left hand over the wound in his right side. The flow of blood continued, bubbling heavily through his fingers.

'Take the horses,' Troop yelled at Parsons. 'Head for that gap yonder.'

As Parsons took the reins, leading the animals away, Troop ran across to Fargo. He threw one arm around Fargo's body and helped the man to walk.

'Move, Fargo,' Troop roared. 'Move, or so help me, I'll put a round straight up your ass!'

Bullets were peppering the air with

regularity now. They were bouncing off the rock and flying in all directions. Grey-uniformed figures were slipping through the rock formations behind Troop and Fargo, and with each passing second they were getting into closer range.

Parsons reached the safety of the gap in the rock-face and guided the horses through. Then he turned and set up a steady volley of covering fire. He shot at every figure he could see. His hand was steady and he shot with great accuracy. Three *Rurales* went down. Whether or not they were dead didn't worry Parsons at that juncture. He was only interested in creating difficulty for the opposition.

Troop, half-carrying Fargo, stumbled into the gap. He let Fargo drop and joined Parsons, adding his rifle to that of his partner.

'This is getting to be like the old days,' Parsons said, a grin forming beneath his moustache.

'Oh hell, I hope you ain't goin' to

start in on that crap,' Troop scowled. 'You tell me one more time about the *good times* and the *great days* we had and I'm going over there and join the Rurales.'

'Nolan, you just ain't fun any more,' Parsons said.

'Never was one for keeping my sense of humour when I'm about to get my head blown off.'

Parsons stopped firing long enough to reload his rifle. He pulled away from the gap as a vicious volley of shots ripped splinters of rock from the sides.

'There a way through to the other end?' he asked Troop.

'We'd better hope so,' Troop answered. His face was streaked with powder-smoke stains and his eyes were red. 'Sooner we get out of this the better I'm goin' to feel.'

'You go ahead,' Parsons said. 'I'll keep that bunch busy a while.'

Troop nodded. He bent over Fargo and hauled him to his feet. Fargo made a lot of noise during the process.

'You going to make it, Fargo?' Parsons asked between shots.

'Don't you fret over me,' Fargo mumbled. 'I'll make it, Luke, else I'll die trying.' He chuckled hoarsely at his own joke.

With a deal of cursing and grunting Troop boosted Fargo into his saddle. Then he gathered the reins of all three horses.

'Fargo, you hang on tight, 'cause if you fall off I ain't comin' back for you.'

'Troop, I got a tighter grip to this saddlehorn than a tenderfoot to a whore's tit.'

Troop, his rifle in his right hand, moved off along the narrow gap between the rock walls, coaxing the nervous horses with soothing words.

Luke Parsons edged himself into a better position by the gap and took stock.

The *Rurales* — those he could see — had fanned out in a line facing the gap. They were behind cover, only showing themselves long enough to loose off a shot, most of which were either too high or off to right or left. Parsons thanked whoever had trained the Mexicans into being such poor shots.

During the next ten minutes the exchange of fire became sporadic. The *Rurales* had found themselves comfortable positions and seemed content to stay there. Parsons didn't allow himself to become too complacent. It was entirely possible that other members of the *Rurales* group had worked their way around to the rear of the outlaws' position and were contemplating an attack from there.

Shots sounded from the far end of the gap. Parsons recognized the sound of Troop's rifle. He responded instantly. Drawing back from the gap he made his way to where Troop had gone. It took precious minutes. There was a lot of loose shale and detritus underfoot which made walking difficult. Parsons made the passage as swiftly as possible. Without warning he found himself out in the open. Bright sunlight hurt his eyes. He blinked away the tears.

'Move it, Luke, this ain't a goddam picnic!'

Parsons glanced in the direction of Troop's voice. Troop was mounted up. He was leaning forward, offering the reins of Parsons' horse. Parsons took the reins and swung up on his own mount.

'That way,' Troop said. He was pointing across the shallow basin they were in. There was an opening in the black rock. 'We follow that it should take us clear away from this part of the beds.'

'I hear shooting?' Parsons asked.

Troop only nodded. Over his shoulder Parsons could see two figures sprawled on the black rock. The grey uniforms were stained with blood. More had been splashed onto the rock itself.

'Figured they were being smart tryin' to sneak in the back way.'

Parsons took the reins of his horse.

'Let's go before more of 'em get the same idea.'

They walked their horses across the basin and through the narrow opening in the rocks on the far side. Now the shooting had stopped the overall silence became ominous.

Parsons, bringing up the rear again, kept throwing glances over his shoulder. He was expecting to see the grey figures slipping through the rocks behind them. And he was sure that someone would start shooting any second. Facing a man with a gun was one thing. It was never easy — but at least it was in front of you. Visible. Offering at least the opportunity of striking back. But this was the worst kind of situation. Where the enemy was unseen and unheard for the most part. Where he could pick his place and time. It left a man feeling naked. Exposed. Left without any kind of a chance. It was the time when the bullet could come from anywhere. At any second. Parsons was sweating heavily and he wished he could rid himself of the itchy spot between his shoulders.

The way ahead opened out. A broad expanse of rock stretched before them. Above the furthest rim blue sky shimmered with heat.

'Now we ride,' Troop said.

They mounted up and moved across the rock. Troop held Fargo's horse close to the rear of his own. From where Parsons was sitting he could see the ragged wound in Fargo's side. It looked bad. The bullets had splintered rib bones, shoving broken edges through the lacerated flesh. Blood was still oozing from the wound. Parsons cursed the situation that was forcing them to keep moving at a time they should have been attending to Fargo's wounds. The way Fargo was losing blood he wasn't going to get very far.

They had covered close on a mile when Parsons picked up a faint shout way behind them. He hunched round in his saddle and saw riders picking their way through the rocks a good quarter mile back.

'They've picked us up again, Nolan!' he said.

Troop had a look, smiling thinly. 'Was starting to think we'd lost 'em.'

'They ain't about to give up.'

'Neither am I,' Troop said.

A few times during the next half-hour rifle shots echoed across the lava-beds. The Mexicans, realizing that their quarry had gained a good distance on them, tried to bring them down with long-range shooting. All they did was to use up a little more ammunition.

'Hey, Nolan, when are we going to get out of this damn place? Parsons asked. 'Sooner we hit real country . . . '

Fargo, who had been riding almost bent double, slithered loosely from the back of his horse. He landed on the rock in a loose sprawl, almost as if his body was devoid of bones. Parsons dismounted and bent over Fargo, turning him on his back.

'He dead?' Troop asked.

Parsons nodded. He unbuckled Fargo's gunbelt and removed it from the body. He tossed it to Troop who hung it from his saddlehorn. Moving to Fargo's horse Parsons removed the canteen. He took what food lay in Fargo's saddlebags and placed it in his own, along with a box of rifle cartridges he found.

'You want the rifle?' Troop asked.

Parsons shook his head. 'Never did like the way it shoots to the left.' He loosened the saddle and dumped it, then removed the bridle. He whacked the horse on the rump. 'Get out of here you asshole.'

Mounting up Parsons kicked his horse into motion.

'Come on, Nolan,' he yelled. 'Let's see if we can shake those goddam greasers out of our hair.'

10

Reining in before the *cantina* Jim climbed stiffly out of the saddle, conscious of the hostile eyes watching every move he made. There were a number of Mexicans lounging outside the *cantina*, all clad in the grey uniform of the *Rurales*. Jim had heard stories about the Mexican law force. This was his first contact with them and it was setting up to be an unpleasant meeting. He'd ridden straight into the waiting guns of three *Rurales* on the outskirts of Valerio. They had disarmed him, using the hard butts of their rifles to hurry him along when he'd moved too slow for them. Then they had ridden him into Valerio. He stood beside his horse, wondering what they had in store for him, determined not to do anything that might provoke them.

One of the three who had brought

him into Valerio approached Jim. The Mexican gestured with the muzzle of his rifle towards the door of the *cantina*, indicating that he wanted Jim to enter. Jim walked in through the door, feeling the cooler air of the interior close around him. The long, low-ceilinged room was deserted save for a uniformed man sitting at one of the tables. As Jim stepped through the door this man raised a hand and beckoned him.

The Mexican who had brought Jim into the *cantina* spoke in rapid Spanish to the seated man. During this time the man at the table kept his eyes fixed firmly on Jim's face. When he spoke it was in clear English.

'You do not understand what has just been said?'

Jim shook his head. 'No.'

'Then we will speak in your tongue.' The man leaned forward. 'I am Captain Melendez.'

'Jim Travis.'

Melendez frowned slightly. 'A name I

am not familiar with.'

'I wouldn't have expected you to know me.'

'I assumed I knew all the members of Luke Parsons' outlaw band.'

Jim gave a thin smile. 'Captain, you've got it all wrong.'

'I have, *Señor?* Perhaps you can correct me then.'

'Easy done. First off — I ain't one of Parsons' boys.'

'Do not take me for a fool, Travis. Why do you think we have been waiting here in Valerio?'

'I don't know why, Captain Melendez. Tell me why.'

'I am not in the mood for games, Travis. You know as well as I that Valerio has long been a haven for the Parsons' outlaw band. Those days are over. They ended two days ago when three of the outlaws reached here. We were waiting for them. Unfortunately they spotted my men and rode away. We gave chase and killed one of them, and I also lost a number of men. The other two eluded us in the lava-beds and then rode north towards the border. I decided to stay here in Valerio in the hope others of the band might show up.'

'I hate to spoil your plans, Captain, but I'm not one of them. Hell, *I'm* chasing Parsons myself.'

Melendez sighed. 'That is so easy to say. Should I allow you to just ride on then?'

'I hope you do, Captain, because if Parsons has jumped back over the border you can't touch him. But I can. I've trailed him all the way down here and I'd hate to lose him now.'

'Tell me why.'

'What brought you to Valerio?'

'News reached us that Parsons and his band had robbed an American bank. Always before they would return to Mexico and come to Valerio.'

'That bank was in Sweetwater in my part of the country, Captain. Part of the money they took from that bank was mine. Hard-earned money. The only way I'm ever going to get that money back is to take it from Luke Parsons. That's why I been trailing him'.

Melendez studied Jim closely. 'The one we killed was named Fargo. Parsons himself and one called Troop escaped. There are still three others not accounted for.'

'Sheriff Tyree back in Sweetwater put a bullet in one of the gang during the robbery. Parsons left him in the mountains 'cause he was slowing the bunch up. I come across him and we shot it out. I buried him on the mountain. I met up with Will Loomis and Lee Brown in some town close to the border. They jumped me first and gave me one hell of a beating 'cause I'd been asking questions all over town about Luke Parsons. Later we had us another run in. Only this time they come out shooting. I was lucky. I stopped one of their bullets. Loomis is dead. Lee Brown is in jail with one of my bullets in him.' Jim paused for a moment, his anger starting to rise. 'And that, Captain Melendez, is the damn truth. You believe it or do what the hell you like, 'cause I'm tired of being kicked around.'

Melendez considered for a moment. He spoke to the man who had brought Jim in. The man turned and left the *cantina*, leaving Jim alone with Melendez. The Mexican stood up and gestured towards a chair.

'I think you had better be seated, *Señor* Travis,' he said. His tone was distinctly softer.

Jim slumped into a seat. He was grateful for the chance to take the weight off his feet. The long ride down into Mexico had been hard on him. The wound in his side had been aching most of the time, and he had felt every jolt from every step his horse had taken. Doc Quincey had been right. Jim had left his bed too soon.

'I believe your story, Travis,' Melendez said. 'It could only be true. You are a very courageous man. These outlaws are wild animals. They have no respect for the laws of man or God.'

'I don't know about that,' Jim said. 'All I want is what they stole from me. Nothing else. I ain't about to let it go.'

'This money they have taken. It is what you have worked for? Earned with your own sweat?'

'Five years of my life is what it's taken to get that money together. It's as simple as that. No way I can let any man walk off with five years of my life.'

'*Si!*' Melendez nodded. 'This I can understand, It is a matter of pride. Of honour.'

It's three thousand damn dollars, Jim thought. But he didn't say any more because Melendez was rapidly becoming even more friendly and Jim wanted to keep things that way.

'When will you ride on?' Melendez asked. 'There are no more one or two hours of daylight left.'

'I'll make a start come morning.'

Melendez smiled. 'Good. Then you can eat with me tonight. I am tired of my own company.' He made a sweeping gesture with his arm. 'Those peasants out there can do no more than ride horses and shoot guns, neither very well. Not one of them can hold a conversation.'

'Well, I ain't all that good myself,' Jim said. 'I can run cows and I know horses. That's about it.'

'You favour horses?' Melendez smiled. 'I also know about horses. We will talk of them tonight.'

And talk they did. Over their meal and well into the night. Melendez *did* know horses. His enthusiasm was boundless. They talked and argued and when it seemed they had exhausted the subject one of them would pick up on some other aspect and the talk would rise again. When Jim did eventually turn in he fell into a deep, sound sleep and didn't wake until bright sunlight caught his face.

'If you ride with us,' Melendez said over a quick breakfast, 'we can show you where Parsons and Troop left the lava-beds and rode north.'

They reached the spot by mid-morning. The trail was faint but it was enough for Jim to follow.

'I wish you luck,' Melendez said. He took Jim's hand. 'Take care, Jim Travis.'

'Thanks for your help.'

'It will be thanks enough to know we have heard the last of the likes of Luke Parsons. Mexico has enough troubles of her own.' He paused. 'And maybe a few friends.'

Jim nodded. 'We can all do with those.'

He took his horse off to the north, looking back some while later to see the straggly line of uniformed *Rurales* riding west, Melendez sitting ramrod straight in his saddle.

★   ★   ★

He camped that night in a dry wash, eating cold because he didn't want to risk a fire. The day's ride had left him stiff and sore. He knew he was pushing his body too hard. Not allowing his

135

wounds time to heal. The trouble was he didn't have time to spare on such luxuries. He needed to close the distance between himself and Luke Parsons. He'd been lucky up to now in that Parsons had been unable to do anything with the money from the robbery except carry it with him. If Parsons managed to find time he might easily hide the money so he could return and pick it up some time in the future. If that did happen recovering it could prove even more difficult than it was already. Jim's best chance — his only chance — was to reach Parsons *before* any thoughts of hiding the money occurred to the outlaw.

★   ★   ★

Jim crossed the border late in the afternoon of the following day. The trail led off slightly to the west now. Ahead lay bare sandstone hills and beyond, purple against the lowering sky, ranged higher, jagged mountains. A faint dry wind drifted across the dusty land-scape. Jim urged his horse forward, his red-rimmed eyes studying the faint tracks.

He had ridden no more than a couple of miles when something caused him to rein in. He leaned forward to get a clearer view of the new sets of tracks and a silent curse passed his lips.

He was looking at the tracks of a group of riders.

Eight — maybe nine of them. The tracks were following those left by Parsons and Troop.

There was something else.

The horses of the trailing riders were unshod.

And in this part of the territory that meant only one thing.

Apaches.

11

He rode through the empty foothills
and on towards the silent mountain
slopes, increasingly aware of the danger
of his situation. The night before he had
camped at the base of a high rock
outcropping, denying himself the comfort of a fire for the second time.
Towards midnight he had picked up the
distant rattle of gunfire. The sounds had
come down out of the high mountains
beyond his camp. Jim had rolled out of
his blanket, moving to where he could
see the black shapes of the high peaks
silhouetted against the night sky. He
had wondered who was doing the
shooting. The Apaches? Parsons and
Troop? It made little difference. Come
morning he still had to ride up there.
The presence of the Apaches made no
difference. He wasn't about to abandon
his claim to that stolen money now. Not

after all the time and trouble it had taken to get this far.

The higher he got the more difficult became the terrain. The early slopes of the mountains were sparsely dotted with greenery. There were a few stunted trees and brush. For the most part it was rock. Crumbling, loose talus slopes footing the sheer rockfaces he was forced to search until he found a way that would allow him to reach the next crest. The ride was slow. The sun was high, moving with infinite slowness across the burnished sky. There wasn't a cloud in sight — or a breath of wind to relieve the oppressive heat. Jim was forced to stop at regular intervals to allow his horse a chance to rest.

By the middle of the afternoon he was above the foothills, trailing through deep canyons and skirting the edges of deep ravines. Towering rockfaces flanked him on both sides. He was finding it increasingly difficult to spot the tracks he was following. The hard rock failed to retain the marks of passing horses, save for the occasional streak where an iron shoe had burred the surface.

He saw where the trail drifted down towards the dry bed of some long-extinct river. Jim took his horse down the dusty, crumbling bank and along the cracked channel. The river had obviously wound its way down from the higher slopes of the mountain during its life. Now all that remained was this dusty course.

The shot came suddenly. The whip-crack report flat and solid, Jim felt something tug at his shirt, over the ribs on the left side. There was a flash of pain. He kicked free of the stirrups and threw himself out of the saddle. As he hit the ground he snatched his gun from the holster.

He lay still. The sound of the shot quickly faded. Silence fell again. Somewhere he could hear the muted sound of his horse picking its way along the river bed. There was nothing else. No sound or movement. But Jim knew that somewhere close by was a man with a gun. He would be watching Jim — and waiting.

Like it or not Jim was going to have to play along. Until he knew where his adversary was located there wasn't much he could do.

Sweat beaded on Jim's forehead and trickled down into his eyes. He blinked furiously against the stinging sensation. There was nothing else he could do.

Time passed. Far too slowly for Jim's liking. Ten minutes. Then fifteen. He began to feel a little foolish. Maybe he was alone. Lying in the dust like some damn fool . . .

A faint sound reached his ears. It was off to his left and above him. Jim reckoned it was someone on the rim of the riverbank, maybe twenty-five feet away. He tightened his grip on the sweat-damp handle of the big Colt in his fist and forced himself to stay calm. Another five minutes slid by before he heard sound again. The soft whisper of fine gravel disturbed by light footsteps. He knew now that his unseen assailant was no white man. Only one breed of human animal could move in such a fashion.

Apache.

At the back of his mind he had already given thought to the chance of his man being an Apache. There were not many white men who would sit for twenty minutes before checking to see if they had hit their target. Most who shot from ambush would simply mount up and ride on, not even bothering to take a close look. But not an Apache. They were born and bred fighters and they were far too dedicated not to make sure they had a kill. There was also another factor much more practical, and forced on the Apache by his situation. A dead white man meant a source of supply; there would be weapons, vital in the Apaches' fight for survival. There would also be ammunition, food, clothing, anything and everything a dead man no longer needed. No Apache worth his salt would pass up the chance of adding an extra rifle, or even a revolver to his arsenal.

Jim listened as his would-be killer approached. Even now the man moved with caution. Jim knew there would be a cocked gun aimed at him. Until the Apache was certain that Jim was dead he would treat him as a potential source of danger. That fact was clear in Jim's mind. He knew, too, that when he did make his move it had to be at the right moment. He would get one chance and have to make the best of it. There were no allowances for mistakes.

A shadow fell across the dusty ground. As Jim's eyes registered the fact the shadow became motionless. A flicker of tension grew in him. He could almost see the Apache studying him, the keen, dark eyes flickering across Jim's still body. He slowed his breathing, hardly daring to even move his eyes. He just kept them fixed on that menacing shadow.

The Apache didn't move for a while. When he did he began to circle Jim's body. Jim swore in frustration. One thing he didn't want was the Apache behind him. He watched the moving shadow. In seconds it would be out of his range of vision. He was going to have to make his move *now*. No matter how risky. Once he lost sight of that shadow he had no guarantee he would see it again.

He placed the position of the Apache by the shadow in relation to the sun, judged distance and angle, and then moved without further thought. He twisted over to the right, away from the Apache. As his rolling body faced towards the Apache, Jim's Colt was exposed. He thrust his arm out and upwards, aiming and firing in one fluid motion. Jim's thumb dogged back the hammer and he triggered again, his second shot merging with the single firing of the Apache's rifle. Jim heard the thwack of the bullet as it ploughed into the earth inches from his face. And in that same split-second he saw the Apache; a dark, squat figure in a faded

144

blue shirt and dirty white pants; long black hair held down by a scarlet headband; he caught a quick impression of a high-boned face, lips drawn back in a snarl of anger. Then his two bullets hit. The first punched a ragged hole high in the Apache's broad chest, passing through the body to emerge from the back of the neck in a gout of blood. The second bullet took the Apache's lower jaw off, jerking his head to one side with a vicious snap.

The moment he had triggered the second shot Jim rolled away from the spot, coming quickly to his feet. He ran for the first cover he spotted, throwing himself down behind a shelf of rock. Twisting his body round he searched the area. He saw nothing. Heard nothing. There was only the dead Apache, an awkwardly sprawled figure on the dusty ground.

Jim stayed where he was for a while, searching the surrounding terrain. He decided finally that the Apache had been on his own. If there had been others he would have heard from them by now. On the other hand he could be wrong. Maybe there *were* others out there. Just waiting for him to show himself. Jim spent a little time replacing the spent cartridges in his revolver. It gave him something to do while he was thinking. True, he had seen the tracks of some eight to nine Apaches trailing Parsons and Troop. He had also heard that shooting during the night. Which could have meant that the two men he was after were dead. Or that some of the Apaches were dead. It might be that the one he'd just shot was nothing more than a scout checking the backtrail. Apaches were notoriously careful about covering themselves when they got involved in any kind of fight. They always liked to have a back door open in case things went against them. It was one of the reasons why they tended to live to ripe old ages.

He stayed where he was for another half-hour, and then his impatience got the better of him. Jim said to hell with it and stood up. He walked slowly along the riverbed, well aware that he was inviting trouble, but determined to see it through. He found his horse some quarter of a mile along the dry course. It turned its head to look at him and stood patiently while he dragged himself back into the saddle. The effort of hauling himself back onto this horse disturbed the graze in his side where the Apache's bullet had caught him. The nagging pain cleared his dulled mind. Gave him something to concentrate on. Jim turned his horse and rode back along the riverbed until he picked up the tracks he'd been following earlier. He saw that they led up the opposite bank and then continued on the rising trail they had been following before.

Jim put his horse on that same trail. Conscious of the added threat from the Apaches he slid his rifle from the sheath and carried it across the saddle as he rode.

12

'Right now I'd trade that money for a fast horse and a loaded gun!'

Luke Parsons glanced across at Troop. His partner's unshaven face was darkened by an angry scowl. Parsons was starting to get edgy. He didn't like the way Troop was acting. He knew Nolan Troop from way back. Knew the man's moods and what could happen when Troop decided to give in to his vicious temper.

'Hell, Nolan, we've been in worse spots than this. Remember that time in . . .'

'Drop it, Luke, I ain't in the mood for any of your cosy memories. All I know is we're stuck on this goddam mountain without horses. I got a handful of bullets left and a near dry canteen. Your contribution seems to be a pair of saddlebags stuffed with money.'

'What do you expect me to do? Leave it behind? This is what we went into Sweetwater for. Remember?'

'I remember,' Troop said. 'And all we've done since then is go down.'

'I guess we have had some hard luck this time round.'

Troop stared at him. '*Hard luck?* Jesus Christ, Luke, this is the worst deal we've ever been handed.'

'So next time we make sure it goes better.'

'*Hell no!* I were you, Luke, I'd start looking for another partner, because I've had it. If I get out of this alive there ain't going to be any next time.'

Parsons shook his head in disbelief. 'You can't quit, Nolan. We've been together too long.'

'Likely that's the trouble,' Troop said. 'Look at us, Luke. A couple of pissants stuck between a rock and a hard place. Nowhere to go. No friends. No homes or families. Hell, the only people who want us are the ones who keep sticking up those reward dodgers. We ride into some towns they'll shoot us full of holes 'fore we have time to say hello.'

'We ain't done so bad. Why we've had some good times. Spent a heap of money. And it ain't true about not havin' friends.'

'You mean those wore-out whores who charge us double 'cause they know we can't complain about it? Or those sons of bitches who make us pay through the nose for every sack of food we want? Or maybe you're talkin' about those Mex bastards back in Valerio. All the times we've stayed in that village, paying our way and keeping them fat and happy. That was one hell of a friendly thing they did letting the *Rurales* in to pick us off.'

'Maybe they didn't have no choice,' Parsons said.

'Luke.'

'Yeah?'

'Shut your goddam mouth.'

Parsons peered out over the top of the rock he was sheltering behind. The long slope that fell away from where they were lying in concealment looked as empty as it had for the last few hours. He knew, though, that the remaining members of the Apache raiding party were still out there somewhere. Parsons' reckoning said there should be no more than four of them left. Trouble was it got harder to tell. The Apaches moved about all the time. Never stayed in one place too long. It tended to become confusing after a while. Since the Apaches had first hit them it had been one long running fight. Troop had lost his horse during the first skirmish. They had ridden double after that — until Parsons' horse had stuck its foot in a hole, spilling the pair to the ground. Troop had snatched up a canteen and Parsons, without conscious thought, had taken the saddlebags holding the money from the Sweetwater raid. After that they had just run, with Apache bullets peppering the air around them. The hours that followed had blurred into a non-stop skirmish, with each side striving to outwit the other. The Apaches were out for blood. Parsons and Troop were simply trying to stay alive. They were well equipped for doing just that. Their existence on the wrong side of the law meant that they spent their lives fighting to stay alive. All that was different this time was the enemy.

In fits and starts, dodging from one place of cover to the next, the pair of fugitives moved ever higher up the barren, rocky slopes of the mountain, struggling to keep the Apaches at bay. The conflict continued spasmodically through the day and into the night. There was a brief lull during the middle hours. As the first fingers of daylight streaked the sky the Apaches began to move again, their closeness showing that they had used the darkness to their advantage.

'Here they come,' Troop muttered. He had spotted one shadowlike figure slipping from rock to rock on the slope below. He let the Apache come on, waiting until the man was in clear sight before he triggered a single shot from his rifle. The shot broke the dawn silence, rattling across the desolate rocky slopes. The bullet took the Apache in the chest, spinning him off his feet. As he hit the ground, arching in pain, the Apache was hit by a second bullet. He flopped over on his face, his body wriggling as ruined nerves reacted to the damage inflicted by Troop's bullets.

The shots seemed to be taken as a signal. A number of guns opened up, bullets howling and whining off the rocks around Parsons and Troop. Slivers of stone filled the air. Razor-sharp splinters capable of inflicting painful gashes if they caught the flesh.

'*Shit!*' Parsons moaned. He had fired a couple of shots from his rifle and had the weapon seize up on him. He struggled to clear the blockage. In the short time his attention was drawn away from the slope a weaving figure broke from a cluster of rocks off his left and came in a dead run directly at Parsons.

'*Luke!*'

Parsons looked up as Troop's warning yell reached him. He saw the approaching Apache. Half-raised his rifle before realizing it was useless. He tossed it aside and snatched his handgun from its holster. As the gun came up, hammer already going back, the Apache uttered a wild yell and threw the lance he was carrying. The tip of the blade grazed Parsons' left shoulder. He stepped back, the shock of the pain causing him to jerk back on the trigger of his gun. It exploded with a heavy sound, the bullet going wide. The Apache slammed into Parsons and the pair of them hit the ground in a tangle of thrashing arms and legs. Bright sunlight glanced off the blade of the knife the Apache snatched from his waistband. Parsons twisted his body to one side as the knife descended. As the Apache eased away from him, prior to making another slash with the knife,

Parsons struck out with the heavy gun in his hand. The muzzle caught the Apache across the left cheek, opening flesh and exposing the cheekbone. A gout of blood frothed from the wound. Swinging his right leg round Parsons drove his knee into the Apache's side, toppling the Indian off balance. Following through he smashed the heel of his boot against the side of the Apache's head. The blow sent the Apache to his knees, shaking his head in pain. Parsons rolled in the opposite direction, rising on to one knee, and bringing his gun round to bear on the dazed Apache. Parsons fired twice, driving the Apache face down in the dust, blood streaming from the ragged holes in his side.

Yards away Nolan Troop drove a bullet into the body of a moving Apache and saw the man go down.

As Parsons rose unsteadily to his feet he became aware of the silence that had fallen. He stared about him. He seemed to distrust the sudden calm that had fallen over the area. His head moved from side to side, eyes searching every possible place that might be concealing yet another Apache.

'That was a damn fool thing to do,' Troop said abruptly, his tone accusing.

'What?'

'Playing around with that rifle.'

'Thing seized up.' Parsons yelled. He rounded on Troop. 'Just quit riding me, Nolan. Bad enough the way things been going without you keep telling me. Let it lay.'

Troop shrugged. He turned and went to where he'd left the canteen of water. Slinging it over his shoulder he walked away from the scene of the fight and started up the slope. He walked on for a few yards then stopped, glancing over his shoulder.

'You coming?' he asked Parsons.

Luke Parsons had picked up his rifle. He snatched up the saddlebags. 'Yeah, I'm coming,' he said. 'What am I supposed to do? Stay here?'

They walked all through the morning, resting at noon beneath a rock overhang that sheltered them from the sun. After a couple of hours they moved on, carrying the knowledge that there could be more Apaches in the area. It was also possible that any survivor from the party that had attacked them could have carried the news back to another group. There was no way of telling. So all they could do was to keep moving. Get clear of the area as quickly as possible. Their first priority after that was to find fresh horses. Which wouldn't be easy. It had to be done, though. A man on foot in this country wouldn't last for very long.

'Got the son of a bitch!' Parsons said triumphantly.

Troop didn't even break his stride. He spoke over his shoulder as he kept on walking. 'What?'

'Damn cartridge that jammed my rifle.' Parsons tossed the offending object aside. 'Nolan, what you got left?'

'Six in my handgun. Four in my rifle.'

'I've got three for the rifle. Two for my Colt.'

'Don't waste 'em,' Troop said.

'Depends on who we meet up with,' Parsons said. 'We get another bunch of Apaches on our tails there ain't but one thing we can do.'

'I figure if we can clear the ridge yonder by nightfall we'll be safe enough,' Troop said, pointing to the distant high crest. 'I recollect a trading post down on the flats. We should make it by noon tomorrow.'

They *did* make the ridge by nightfall; in fact they topped the ridge with a half-hour to spare. Footsore and weary they started on down the far slopes, walking until sheer exhaustion and a lack of light forced them to halt. They found a sheltered spot and lay down, sleeping like the dead. By first light they were on the move again, having breakfasted on a mouthful of water from the canteen. The day quickly turned out to be as hot as the previous one. They stumbled and slithered down the loose, dusty slopes, suffering bruises and scratches as they came into contact with the keen rocks. Their clothing, shredded and torn, caked with thick dust, clung damply to their sweating, aching bodies. Red-rimmed eyes stared out from faces masked with gritty dust.

Towards noon they clambered up a crumbling bank and slumped to the ground. A half-mile distant they could see the low buildings that made up the trading post. A lazy spiral of smoke curled skywards from a stone chimney. In a corral close by the main building horses milled about restlessly.

'Knew I was right,' Troop muttered; he was speaking more to himself than to Parsons.

'Damn right you were, Nolan,' Parsons grinned.

'Reckon I'll pick me up a good horse and get the hell out of this godforsaken piece of county,' Troop said. He half turned to stare at Parsons. 'I figure to have my share of that money, Luke.'

'Sure, Nolan, whatever you want.'

They walked in to the post and were met by a large, wild-eyed dog that circled them warily, a low rumbling growl rising in its throat. Troop ignored the animal, while Parsons, who had always carried a fear of dogs, trod his way past with extreme caution.

A tall, lean man with a keen-eyed stare, stepped out of the post door and leaned against the adobe wall. He glanced from Troop to Parsons, shrewdly assessing their position.

'Be foolish to think you boys were on foot 'cause you like walkin',' he said.

'Apaches,' Troop told him, jerking a thumb in the direction of the distant peaks. 'Got one horse shot from under us. The other put its foot in a damn hole.'

The lean man nodded. 'You boys could be in luck. Got some horses over in the corral there for sale. Bought 'em from the army agent last week. I can let you have 'em for a fair price.'

'We'll take a look later,' Troop said. 'Could do with a meal first. Ain't eaten decent for a spell.'

'Come on in, boys, and make yourselves to home. We might not have the best food in the territory but there's plenty of it.'

'Coffee,' Troop said as they tramped inside. 'Hot and black and sweet.'

'Sure.'

There was a long wooden table set near one wall. All around them the interior of the post building was stacked with goods of every description. The air was heavy with the aroma of coffee. Of leather and spices. The tang of tobacco. Troop and Parsons trailed after the lean man. He pointed in the direction of the table.

'Set,' he said. 'I'll fetch some coffee.'

Parsons sank onto one of the wooden benches. He let the saddlebags slip to the floor at his feet. A great weariness flooded over him. He had never felt so tired in his life before. He leaned back and closed his eyes.

'*Get this down, Luke.*'

He sat upright with a jerk. His eyes

snapped open and he saw Troop pushing a mug of steaming coffee at him. Parsons took the mug and gulped a mouthful of the sweet, black brew. He felt it burn its way down to his stomach.

'Nolan, did you mean what you said out there?' he asked.

Troop poured himself more coffee. 'I meant it.'

'Jesus, Nolan, why?' Parsons struggled to find words he could use to convince Troop he was making a mistake. 'What the hell are we going to do if we quit?'

'Live a lot longer maybe,' Troop said.

'I can't see you sittin' in a rocking-chair on some front porch,' Parsons said.

'It's got to be better than getting shot to pieces in some no account town.'

'It doesn't have to be that way,' Parsons argued. 'We stick together we can beat anything they send against us.'

'Face it, Luke, it ain't the same. We ain't gettin' any younger and the banks are harder to bust. Hell, look at us now.

There's only you and me left.'

'I know we lost Fargo. But Bristow was alive when we left him on that mountain. And the others'll join up with us somewhere.'

'I don't think so, Luke. I've got a feeling they ain't coming.'

'Nolan, I never heard you talk like this before.'

Troop shrugged his wife shoulders. 'Likely because I never felt this way before. Can't tell you why. All I do know is I want out. I need some peace and quiet. Some place where I can forget about this kind of mess. No more having to move on all the time. No more being chased from hell to breakfast. Being shot at. Going hungry. I've done enough of that. It's time to quit, Luke, and that's what I aim to do.'

Their food arrived. Plates piled high with thick slices of beef and browned potatoes, spiced beans and gravy. It was brought to the table by a silent, dark-eyed Indian squaw. The lean man followed her to place knives and forks on the table.

'How you boys doing?'

'Fine,' Parsons said.

'Yell if you want anything,' the man said. 'The names Jonas, by the way.'

Troop glanced at him silently. He saw Jonas's face darken slightly; as if the man had realized he was treading dangerous ground.

'Mind, I never pay much heed to names myself. If a man *wants* to tell me, that's fine. If he doesn't . . . well, that's his business I guess.'

Jonas backed off, disappearing into the depths of the post. Parsons and Troop ate their meal without another word being passed between them. Both had their thoughts, their private fears for what might lie ahead.

Some time later Jonas walked by the table and stepped outside. His manner aroused Troop's curiosity. He stood up and moved to one of the windows looking out over the yard. He stayed at the window for a while. He seemed to be watching something going on outside.

'What's wrong, Nolan?' Parsons asked. He had paused in the act of pouring himself more coffee.

Troop moved back from the window. He picked up his rifle and made sure there was a shell in the breech.

'Damnit, Nolan, what is it?'

'Rider coming in,' Troop said evenly.

'You'd kind of expect that at a place like this.'

'This ain't no damn passer by,' Troop said. 'He looks like he's been riding a long time. And he's comin' in from the same direction we did.'

'You recognise him?' Parsons asked. He reached for his own rifle.

'No. But I'm sure the son of a bitch has been trailing us. He must want something pretty bad.'

Parsons had placed the saddlebags holding the money from the Sweetwater bank on the table. 'If it's this he's come after he's going to have to kill me to get it.'

'Could be that's on his mind.'

'You figure he's a lawman?'

Troop shrugged his shoulders and strode to the door, pushing past the man called Jonas. He stepped outside and positioned himself against the wall. His rifle was held loosely in one hand, against his leg; unobtrusive yet ready for instant use.

'You expecting company?' Jonas asked.

Troop shifted his weight from one foot to the other. 'I'm always expecting certain kinds of company,' he said, then turned his attention to the rider coming around the far end of the corral.

13

Jim's horse paced steadily across the dusty yard fronting the trading post. Sighting the tall man as he stepped out of the door, Jim had drawn his right hand close to the butt of his holstered Colt. He was aware of the intensity of the man's stare; there was an aura of extreme violence barely held in check. It radiated from the man with an almost physical force. Jim knew without being told that he was facing Nolan Troop. Tyree's description of the man was exact, and Jim recalled what Sweetwater's lawman had told him about Troop's reputation; he was a hard man, with little regard for any life save his own; if someone got in his way Troop would sweep him aside without a moment's thought.

There was a second man in sight. He was standing close to the post door. Tall and lean Jim saw; certainly not Luke Parsons. By his clothing Jim judged him to belong to the trading post.

So where the hell is Parsons?

Jim glanced to either side. Nothing. There wasn't much in the way of cover. The buildings of the post all lay before him. Parsons was likely to be there somewhere. Maybe even inside the post itself.

He'll show himself when he's ready, Jim decided. There was nothing to be gained from getting too worried because he couldn't see both men. They weren't going to make it easy for him.

'That's close enough,' Troop called out.

Jim reined in, settling his gaze on Troop.

'What's your business here, *boy?*'

'To do with something that belongs to me,' Jim said.

He felt his anger rising at the way Troop had called him boy, but he fought it down as he realized that Troop was trying to rattle him. Once he became aware of that fact he was able to restrain himself.

'Spit it out, boy,' Troop snapped.

'Three thousand dollars of the money you took from Sweetwater is mine,' Jim told him, surprised at his calmness.

Troop grinned. He seemed amused at Jim's statement. 'Hell, boy, least you've made my day.'

'Troop, it wasn't that funny, and I'm not laughing, *mister*.'

'Don't get smart with me, boy, else I'm liable to forget what a good mood I'm in.' Troop moved away from the post a distance. 'You follow us from Sweetwater?'

'All the way,' Jim said evenly.

Troop studied him. 'What happened to your face?'

'Ran into some of your friends.'

Troop's grin vanished. 'Loomis? Brown? Where are they, boy?'

'Brown's teamed up with a US Marshal. Mind it'll only last as long as it takes to reach the nearest jail.'

'Loomis?'

'He's dead, Troop. He tried to kill me. He didn't make it.'

'*You* took Will Loomis?' Troop shook his head in disbelief. 'What did you do — backshoot him?'

Jim refused to rise to Troop's bait. 'I figure that kind of play would be more in your line, Troop. Same as shooting down a lone man trying to get back his stolen horses. You remember John Mulchay?'

'He should have cut his losses.'

'I'll tell him that next time I see him.'

'He still alive?'

'Far as I know. Looks like you boys are having a spell of bad luck. I'd say it's running out fast.'

'Well, don't you fret on it,' Troop said, his voice taking on a hard edge. 'And don't get any ideas about me handing back any damn money, boy, 'cause things can change. I've got a feeling my luck's on the turn.'

'Troop, all I'm interested in is my three thousand dollars. You do what the hell you like with the rest of it. I've ridden a damn long way and been kicked seven ways from Sunday, and I ain't about to ride out of here until this is settled one way or the other.'

'You've either got guts, boy, else you're plain crazy.'

'Some of both I reckon,' Jim said.

'Well I'll give it to you straight. You turn that horse about and ride out and do it now. That way you might stay alive. Keep pushing I'm just going to have to kill you.'

Jim watched Troop's face. The man's eyes were fixed. Unblinking. An expression of momentary weariness clouded his features. As if he was reluctantly forcing himself to initiate a course of action that could only end in a violent confrontation.

And then the expression changed. The eyes sharpened. Focused. The line of the mouth hardened.

Troop's right hand swept the rifle away from his leg, the muzzle rising to line up on Jim's body.

Realizing he had no more than a scant few seconds Jim acted out of pure survival instinct. His left hand dragged down on the rein, pulling his horse's head aside. In the same instant he drove his heels deep into the horse's sides, catching the animal by surprise. The startled animal lunged forward, following its head, and was forced to veer to the left.

The muzzle of Troop's rifle spat a gout of flame and powdersmoke.

Jim snatched his handgun from the holster, thumb dogging back the hammer as he slid his boots from the stirrups and let himself fall from the saddle.

Troop, seeing his shot had missed, worked another round into the breech.

The ground rushed up to meet Jim. He thrust out a hand to break his fall, then took the reduced impact on his shoulder. Tucking in his head he let himself be carried forward in a roll. He twisted his body round, pushing his gunhand out ahead of him.

As Jim's horse raced on by him, leaving a cloud of dust in its wake, Troop ran forward, cursing wildly as the dust hid Jim for a brief few seconds. It was enough for Jim. He touched the trigger and felt his gun slap against his palm as it fired. A mist of dust spurted from Troop's shirt where the bullet hit. Troop stumbled slightly, regained his balance, turning in Jim's direction. His rifle's muzzle sagged groundwards. Troop jerked the weapon level, firing a fraction of a second too soon; his bullet gouged through the hard-packed dirt inches from Jim. In the few seconds since firing his first shot, Jim had cocked his gun again, and even as Troop's bullet was kicking up the dirt, Jim returned the shot. This time Troop went down, his body twisting in agony as he hit the hard ground. Yet he refused to stay down, dragging his legs under his body to thrust himself to his knees. His left hand was clamped over the bloody wound in his body. He jammed the stock of his rifle against his hip and worked the lever one-handed, tilting the muzzle up to meet Jim's body as he climbed to his feet.

'Leave it, Troop!' Jim yelled; he didn't want to kill the man, but was fast realizing that Troop had no intention of backing off, no matter how badly hurt he was.

'Go to hell, you son of a bitch,' Troop snarled through bloody lips. He braced a foot against the ground and hauled himself upright. 'I ain't about to get took by no . . . '

Two guns fired as one, the combined sound slapping against the hot silence that surrounded the isolated trading post.

Jim braced himself for the impact of a bullet that never came.

Yards away Nolan Troop was thrown flat on his back by Jim's bullet. It caught him directly over the heart. He was dead before his discarded rifle hit the ground.

Jim's hands were trembling as he flipped open the loading gate of his gun and ejected the spent shell cases. He thumbed in fresh loads and then he walked towards the post.

Jonas, who had stood rooted to the spot during the brief gun fight, stepped aside as Jim neared him. He was no coward, but he had seen the hard gleam in Jim's eyes, and he knew enough not to interfere with him.

'Where is he?' Jim asked as he neared the door.

'He *was* inside 'fore I stepped out. The other one,' jerking a thumb in the direction of Nolan Troop, 'followed me straight off.'

Jim nodded. He stepped in through the door, blinking his eyes as he was met by the comparative darkness inside the building. He stepped by the open door.

Heard the dry creak of its hinges as it was moved.

A shadow moved close to him.

Jim half-turned. Saw a dark shape rush at him. As he became aware of his exposed position he tried to step aside.

He was too late. Something hard clouted him across the back of the shoulders. The pain made him gasp. He was knocked off balance by the blow. He threw up a hand to try to ward off any further attack. It didn't save him. He heard a man grunt with effort. The back of his head seemed to burst apart under the savage blow that came out of nowhere. The darkness around him blazed with brilliant light for a few pain-filled seconds, and then the darkness returned. Jim felt himself falling forward. He thought of the floor and threw out both hands to break his fall. But contact with the floor never came. He just kept right on falling. Into endless, silent, enveloping darkness.

14

'Boy, it's lucky you've got a hard head,' Jonas said.

'It's being hard-headed that got me into this mess,' Jim told him ruefully. 'Trouble is I never learn by my mistakes.'

He was seated at the very same table Parsons and Troop had used. Now Nolan Troop was dead, and Luke Parsons, after beating Jim unconscious, had taken a horse from Jonas and had made his escape.

'You want more coffee?' Jonas asked.

Jim pushed his cup across the table, resisting the urge to nod. He was attempting to stay as still as possible until the savage aching in his head subsided. True, the pain wasn't as bad as it had been on recovering consciousness. At that time Jim had wondered if Parsons had hit him so hard it might leave some permanent damage. The thought had left him in a cold sweat. Then the pain had eased some and he had just taken things easy, one step at a time, allowing his senses to recover.

'Now I ain't a man who normally holds a grudge,' Jonas said abruptly, 'but I'm ready to make an allowance for that son of a bitch. Hell, I draw the line at bein' held at gunpoint in my own place, an' then having to saddle up a horse for *him* to steal.'

'And ideas to where he's heading?' Jim asked.

'Direction he took's liable to fetch him up in the high country,' Jonas said. 'Way it looked to me he wasn't too particular which way he went. He was getting real jumpy. You've got him scared, boy, no doubt about it.'

'You think *he's* scared?' Jim picked up the refilled cup of coffee.

Jonas chuckled softly. 'I know what you mean. Been scared a few times myself. Mind I'm old enough to know it don't matter none. Bein' scared of something is as natural as breathin'. Means you're aware of what's going on around you. Man who says he ain't afeared of anything is a damn liar — and a fool to boot.'

'Isn't he still a fool if he knows what he's getting into but still goes on?'

'Talking about yourself? Hell, boy, there are times when a man just don't have any choice. He can step back an' take a look at what he's doing, but it don't make any difference. He still has to keep right on doing it. I figure it's the difference between being a man or not having the sand to face up to whatever life has to throw at you. Back down once and you'll likely end up doin' the same thing every time there's trouble.'

'Gets kind of monotonous, though,' Jim said. 'Seems every time I take a step forward I get knocked back a half dozen.'

'Bide your time, boy, and you'll get there.'

'I need a fresh horse, Mr. Jonas,' Jim

179

said. 'You willing to do me a trade?'

'No problem.' Jonas grinned. 'And I'll make sure *you* don't get no crowbait.'

'Meaning?'

'Parsons don't know it yet, but he ain't going to get too good a ride out of that horse he took.'

'Something wrong with it?' Jim asked.

'Could be. That animal has a weak foreleg. If Parsons pushes it too hard it's going to fall down on him.'

'You knew about it?'

'Sure. But I didn't feel inclined to let Parsons know. What with his gun pokin' in my ear and all — I guess it slipped my mind.'

Jim found himself grinning widely. 'Mr. Jonas, I guess it must have done just that.'

★　★　★

Jonas did more than provide a fresh horse. He made sure Jim had everything he needed from food to ammunition.

He even threw in a heavy sheepskin coat.

'It can get pretty cold on those high peaks,' he explained.

'Thanks,' Jim said.

'You just keep your eyes peeled, boy, 'cause Parsons is on his own now. He's going to be real nervous. Ready to shoot at anything that moves. Just be careful and don't trust a damn thing he does.'

'I'll keep that in mind.'

'I were you, boy, I'd get it done — then maybe think about it. Luke Parsons ain't about to allow you the luxury of taking your time. Come the day he's going to play it mean and sneaky.'

★　★　★

He rode out from the trading post and trailed north. Parsons' tracks were easy to follow. The outlaw was riding hard and fast, making no attempt to conceal his trail. He was either too concerned with getting clear of the area, or becoming careless because he was running scared. It made little difference as far as Jim was concerned. He knew he was close to Luke Parsons now. He had no intention of allowing the man to slip away a second time.

A couple of hours of steady riding brought Jim to the first of the rising slopes marking the foothills. The skyline ahead was dominated by the sheer bulk of the gaunt peaks. Jim put his horse up the rocky slopes, his eyes constantly searching the way ahead. Parsons' tracks petered out every so often, mainly because he was keeping to the hard bedrock whenever it showed, and Jim lost some time as he searched for the trail.

Late in the day he spotted a good campsite and decided to get some rest. It was too risky to go blundering around the treacherous slopes in the dark. Jim made himself a good fire this time. He was getting tired of making cold camps. He cooked a meal and brewed a pot of coffee. He ate slowly, reflecting a little sourly that it was a miserable way to be existing. Here he was, all on his own, stuck out on the slopes of some inhospitable mountain range. The way things were running the only definite prospect ahead of him was the likelihood of being shot at. And for what? A bundle of dollars . . .

Jim sat upright. His food became suddenly tasteless. It was the first time he'd even *considered* that what he was doing might be wrong. He pushed his plate aside and stared into the darkness beyond his lonely camp. *Why had he suddenly entertained such a thought?* Possibly because he'd been too busy previously to give it much attention. Too busy trying to stay alive. Now though he was able to think about the men who had died. The wounded outlaw abandoned on the mountain. His meeting with that man seemed a lifetime ago. Then there had been Loomis and Brown; Loomis was dead, Brown was in jail. And then there had been Nolan Troop. Jim's three thousand dollars was coming high. *Too high?* Did the return of his money justify the deaths of three men? Jim stirred restlessly. He poured himself a mug of coffee, trying to find answers to the questions crowding his confused mind. The answers refused to come. He felt angry, and for the first time since leaving Sweetwater, he felt unsure of himself and his motives. Maybe he was tired. A good night's sleep might help to clear the confusion. Somehow he didn't think it would. He sat staring into the flames of his fire, and the longer he sat the heavier became his misgivings. After a time a new image grew in his mind. It was of Jenny. He realized he could easily forget about everything, maybe even his money, when he thought about her. He admitted that he wanted to be back with her. Able to see her. Touch her . . .

The click of a gun hammer going back drove deeply into Jim's silence. His right hand dropped to the butt of his Colt, fingers brushing the smooth wood.

'*Leave it, boy, or I'll blow your damned head clear off!*'

Jim took his hand from his gun. He tried to locate the position of the speaker but the darkness beyond his fire gave nothing away.

'Set easy, boy, 'cause I'm primed to touch this trigger.'

'*Parsons?*'

'Yeah. It's me, you son of a bitch.'

'You want something?' Jim asked. 'Or have you decided to hand back my money?'

'*No way!*' Parsons said. 'That money's mine now, boy, and the hell with you!'

'So what are you here for?'

'I could kill you right now, no trouble. Like steppin' on a bug.'

'Maybe,' Jim answered. His eyes had adjusted to the darkness and he could make out the denser shape of Luke Parsons' crouching form. 'So what's stopping you?'

'I'm ready to give you the chance to back off and stay alive. I ain't about to gain anything from killing you, boy, so get the hell out of here. Go on back where you came from.'

Jim heard the outlaw's words but didn't allow himself to be taken in by Parsons' offer. He couldn't figure out what Parsons was up to. Didn't really care. He just knew that he was at a disadvantage at that precise moment.

He kicked out with his left boot, overturning the pot of coffee into the flames of the fire. A cloud of hissing steam rose as the flames were extinguished, and Jim rolled to one side, clawing for the gun on his hip.

From the darkness came the slam of a gunshot. A lance of flame flickered for a moment. The bullet whacked against the ground close to where Jim had been seconds before.

Turning his head in time to catch the fragment of gunflash, Jim snapped off a couple of hasty shots before getting his feet under him and heading for substantial cover.

'Damn you, boy,' Parsons yelled out of the darkness, 'I ain't finished with you yet.'

The night was split open by another shot from Parsons' gun; this one was impossibly wide of the target.

Jim returned fire again. A single shot — and he heard a muffled curse. He pulled further back from the campsite, his back to a rocky shelf.

'Where are you, boy? Show yourself and we'll finish this now!' Parsons' voice rolled out across the rocky slopes, losing itself in the empty terrain.

Jim held his silence. He could hear Parsons stumbling and rattling around in the dark.

'*Boy? You hear me?*'

Again Jim stayed silent.

Parsons began to mutter to himself. His rising anger eventually burst out in a wild and incoherent howl of rage.

Jim eased away from his position and began to work his way to where he'd left his horse; the realization of the animal's vulnerability had come to him even as Parsons began to give free rein to his anger again.

'*Come on out, boy, and face me!*'

Reaching his tethered horse Jim tugged the halter rope free. The animal had remained calm throughout the shooting and even now it offered no resistance as Jim led it into the deep cluster of rocks just beyond the camp.

'I'm going to find you, boy, come sunup. You made me run, you son of a bitch, and I ain't about to forget that. You hear me, you bastard.'

Pushing his way deep into a dense thicket of brush Jim found a sheltered hollow large enough to take himself and his horse. Tethering the animal Jim settled himself on the hard ground, with his back against the slope of the hollow. He reloaded his handgun and prepared to sit out the night. It wasn't long before the chill of the mountain air penetrated his clothes. Jim thought about the warm campfire he'd been forced to abandon. He thought too of the hot coffee he'd made. He could have done with that right there and then, and the thick coat Jonas had given him. Parsons' appearance had caught him off guard. He had no one to blame but himself. If he hadn't been feeling so sorry for himself he might have ben prepared.

Jim felt some of the old anger return. *Damn Luke Parsons.* If this was the way he wanted to play the game it was fine with Jim Travis. He shivered against the cold. It was going to be a long, uncomfortable night. By morning he was going to be more than ready to face Luke Parsons.

15

Jim moved at first light.

He circled away from his campsite and headed for higher ground, leading his horse. Reaching a higher slope he was able to look down on his campsite. It was deserted. He could see the blackened circle where his fire had been. His cooking utensils were scattered about the area. There were articles of clothing as well. Parsons had ransacked the camp *and* Jim's personal belongings. The sight of his scattered clothing angered Jim more than anything else. He knew he should have been more concerned by the fact that Parsons had probably taken Jim's rifle and the extra ammunition he'd been carrying. That left Jim with just his loaded handgun and the ammunition he had in his belt-loops.

'*Damn you, Luke Parsons,*' Jim said.

He worked his way back down to the vicinity of his wrecked camp. Leaving his horse tethered in some thick brush Jim eased his way in closer. He took his time. It was about the only thing he had plenty of. He studied the camp and the terrain around it for a long time, and didn't move in until he was satisfied Parsons wasn't close by.

Standing over the scorched earth where his fire had been Jim looked the camp over. Parsons had taken everything he could make use of. What he had left behind had been rendered useless; Jim's clothing had been cut to ribbons, his eating utensils crushed underfoot. Even his saddle had been slashed open.

'You bastard,' Jim murmured bitterly. He snatched off his hat and slapped it against his pants leg in pure frustration. 'Damn you to hell!' This time he yelled the words out loud.

He was scanning the slopes above him in that moment, and his eyes caught the brief flicker of light reflecting off metal. For a split second Jim froze. Then turned on his heel and dived across the blackened circle of ashes. As he hit the ground on the far side he heard the slam of a rifle. Heard the whine and whack of the bullet as it ploughed into the earth no more than a foot away. Jim rolled desperately, dust misting the air around him as he bellied across the ground, his gut coiled up in a greasy knot; he was as exposed as a fly in the middle of a dinner plate. The high slopes echoed to the rattle of gunshots as the rifleman loosed off shot after shot, a line of bullets chewing up the earth in Jim's wake.

He reached the far side of the campsite, recalling a shallow gully, choked with brush. The night before he had gathered the fuel for his fire from it. Now, without a moment's hesitation, Jim plunged over the edge, his body cartwheeling down the crumbling bank. He crashed into the tangle of brush at the bottom and fetched up on the gully floor with a solid thump. He lay for a while, his body aching, chest heaving as he tried to drag air into his starved lungs. He sat up. The shooting had stopped. Jim climbed to his feet, shouldering his way through the thick brush. He worked his way along the gully until he was some fifty yards away from the campsite. Crawling up the dusty side of the gully he peered over the lip, his eyes searching the slopes above him.

At first there didn't seem much to see. Just the crumbling slopes of rock, dotted with the odd clump of brush. Maybe Parsons had moved on. Retreated into the depths of the mountain. Or perhaps he was working his way down to Jim's level, intending to carry the fight back to Jim. Whichever it was, Jim decided, he was good and mad enough to face Parsons.

He dragged himself out of the gully, ignoring the aches and pains spreading over his body. His big Colt hung down at his side, his thumb on the hammer ready to ear it back. He walked forward, searching for any sign of Luke Parsons.

Just beyond the gully a wide stream flowed down the slope. Jim paused at its edge. The clear water looked cool and fresh and inviting. For a moment Jim's concentration drifted.

And it was then that Luke Parsons stepped into sight from behind a shelf of rock. He had a rifle in his hands. The moment he set eyes on Jim he swung the rifle in line and pulled the trigger.

Jim heard the click of the hammer fall. His body tensed as he waited for the sound of the shot. Nothing came. He saw the expression in Parson' eyes, realized that the outlaw's weapon had misfired, and brought up his Colt. The hammer was back well before the muzzle settled on Parsons and Jim's finger touched the trigger.

Parsons had already dropped the rifle, his right hand reaching for his own handgun.

Jim could have completed his pull on

the trigger to drive a shot at the outlaw, but his finger froze. He knew in that moment that he had no desire to kill Luke Parsons.

'*Leave it!*' Jim yelled. He angled the Colt's muzzle so it was aimed directly at Parsons' head. 'Even I couldn't miss this close.'

Luke Parsons took his eyes from the unwavering muzzle of Jim's gun and stared at the face behind it. He tried to read the expression in Jim's eyes. What he saw caused him to ease his fingers away from the butt of his gun.

'Use the left hand,' Jim ordered. 'Unbuckle the belt.' He waited until Parsons had done so. 'Now toss it in the water.'

'You . . . '

'*Just do it!*' Jim snapped. 'Now.'

Parsons heaved gun and belt into the stream.

'Now the rifle. Pick it up muzzle first.'

Parsons did as he was told. He watched the rifle sink without dismay.

'Second time that damn thing jammed on me.'

'That leaves just one thing to settle before I take back my money,' Jim said.

'*What?*' Parsons asked. 'Jesus, you want *me* to jump in the goddam water as well?'

Jim unbuckled and removed his gunbelt. Then he calmly unloaded his Colt and tossed the cartridges in the stream before putting the gun aside.

Luke Parsons had watched this with interest. Now his unshaven face creased into a grin.

'Son of a bitch,' he breathed. 'You really mean it, don't you, boy?' He laughed. 'It's really got you mad. The way I ran off with your damn money. Well come on, boy, 'cause I feel the same way on account of how you've been dogging me all the way from that pissant town.'

Jim didn't answer. He simply walked forward, into the water and waded across the stream to where Luke Parsons stood waiting.

As Jim stepped onto his side of the stream Parsons lunged forward, his humour vanishing as he swung a round-house right at Jim's head. His fist met fresh air as Jim stepped easily to one side, then sank his powerful fist deep into Parsons' exposed stomach. A rush of air burst from Parsons' mouth. As he sagged forward Jim's fist sledged round and clouted him on the side of the face, spinning him to the ground. As Parsons struck Jim drove the toe of his boot into the outlaw's side. The sheer force of the blow turned Parsons onto his back Jim followed close, hoping to keep the advantage he'd gained. But he hadn't allowed for Luke Parsons' experience as a brawler. Hurt as he was Parsons responded quickly, and as Jim stepped in, the outlaw lashed out with one of his heavy boots. The sole smashed across Jim's knee. A numbing pain speared up Jim's leg. He felt it give. As Jim went down Parsons' fist met him halfway. It was a savage blow that caught Jim full in the mouth, splitting his lips. Blood spurted instantly. Parsons hit him again, a solid punch that ripped across the side of Jim's jaw. The impact stunned Jim and he lost all touch with reality. When he was able to focus again he was on his back with Luke Parsons standing over him. One of Parsons' boots was swinging in at Jim's head. He threw up both hands, grabbing the boot and twisting hard. Parsons howled in agony as Jim turned the foot against the ankle joint. He was forced to go in the direction Jim was turning the foot, losing his balance and plunging face down in the dirt. In the time it took Parsons to regain his balance Jim climbed to his feet. For a moment they faced each other, weighing the odds, seeking an opening. Jim moved first, launching a right that Parsons blocked, then followed with a punch of his own. It caught Jim in the face, knocking him back a step. Jim braced himself and met Parsons' sudden rush with a brutal fist that crushed the outlaw's nose. A pained grunt burst from Parsons' lips. His face was spattered with blood. He ducked low, driving hard blows to Jim's ribs. Jim grabbed for Parsons' shirt, gripped it, and jerked Parsons in close. He drove his knee up into Parsons' face, catching him on the left cheek. The blow angered Parsons and he began to swing wildly. Most of his punches missed, though enough landed to cause Jim a deal of pain. He responded likewise, and for a time the pair of them traded cruel, damaging blows. Neither gave nor lost any ground. They battered each other relentlessly, putting a great deal of anger and hate and frustration into every punch. When Parsons swung a wild punch that missed Jim saw his chance and landed a heavy blow that took Parsons full in the face. Parsons stumbled back, lost his footing and went into the stream. Jim launched himself forward, his momentum carrying him bodily into the outlaw. They hit the water in a fighting tangle, churning the stream to a bubbling, pink-tinged froth. Gasping for air they smashed blow after blow at each other, fists crushing and splitting flesh. There was little room for mercy or any thought of compromise in their actions. They were both fighting for survival. For personal satisfaction. It was a win or lose conflict for them both. And though Parsons was the heavier and more experienced he was up against a man of unflinching character. A man who refused to allow any odds to deter him. Jim was also a lot younger. His stamina, though flagging, carried him on when Parsons' began to fail. He became aware of Parsons' slower responses. His weaker blows. And Jim made good use of his opponent's lowering resistance. He drove Parsons back to the land, delivering blow after blow at the outlaw's face and body until Parsons went down again — and stayed down.

'*That's it!* Hell, that's it . . . you crazy son of a bitch,' Parsons mumbled through swollen, bloody lips. He coughed harshly, spitting blood. 'Damnit, boy, whatever you wanted out of your system — it's gone.' He flopped back on the ground and lay there, his chest heaving as he fought to drag air into his tortured lungs.

Jim recrossed the stream and picked up his Colt. He put on his gunbelt, finding the task difficult because his fingers were badly swollen. He was beginning to feel sick. His whole body burned with pain and he was bleeding all over the place. He somehow managed to reload his gun, and once he'd done that he returned to where Parsons lay, prodding the outlaw to his feet.

'Take me to it,' he said, every word he uttered causing him great discomfort.

'Boy, I get the feeling if I'd shot you dead you would've still kept coming for that goddam money.'

'You believe that, Parsons,' Jim said. 'It's the truest thing you've said today.'

Parsons' horse was tethered a short distance away. The first thing Jim noticed was his own rifle in the saddle boot. He crossed to the horse and retrieved it.

'Lucky for me you didn't use it,' he said.

'Hell, boy, don't keep reminding me,' Parsons replied peevishly.

'The money?' Jim suggested.

Parsons freed the saddlebags from behind his saddle.

'On the ground,' Jim said. 'You *and* the saddlebags.'

With Parsons on his belly Jim took the outlaw's own saddlerope and tied Parsons' hands behind his back.

'Jesus Christ, boy, you're tyin' that rope awful tight,' Parsons complained.

'I don't aim to give you any damn chance at all.'

'Where we headed?'

'Back to Sweetwater,' Jim told him. 'There're folk who'll jump at the chance to meet you again.'

'Boy, you've got a nasty streak in you that's starting to show.'

'Parsons, I hurt all over. I'm carrying

a fair few nicks and burns I didn't have 'fore I left Sweetwater. It's going to be some time before I look myself again. And you, mister, are the cause of it all. The way I see it whatever can be done to make you uncomfortable, even downright miserable, well that's just fine by me.'

Parsons rolled over and sat up. 'Those pissants back in Sweetwater are liable to string me up, boy.'

Jim glanced up from opening the saddlebags. 'You could just about be right about that.'

He turned the contents of the saddlebags onto the ground. Stared at the wads of crumpled banknotes.

'Hell, boy, there are more dollar bills there than either of us is likely to see again,' Parsons said, his tone low and with a sly edge to it. 'You know what I mean, boy?'

Jim counted off some of the money, folded it and put it in his shirt pocket. He bundled the rest of the money back in the saddlebags and fastened the flaps.

'All I see is three thousand dollars,' he said. 'It's what I came for. It's all I want.'

Luke Parsons didn't say any more. There wasn't much point. You couldn't argue with a man with principles. Parsons was too tired to even think about trying. It was like banging your head against a stone wall; the only good thing to it was when you stopped — but with this man there wouldn't be any stopping. He'd stick to his damn principles until hell froze over, and that could turn out to be a long time coming.

16

Sheriff Tyree had taken an intense dislike to the stick he was hobbling around on. He *knew* it was for his own good. The local doctor kept telling him that. It only made things worse. Tyree just didn't like having to depend on the stick. He couldn't do without it though. His leg wasn't healing as fast as expected. The doc had given a reason for that as well. In plain words it was to the effect that as a man got older he took longer to heal up. Which hadn't done a deal for Tyree's state of mind. The upshot was that he forced himself to take as much exercise as he could in order to strengthen his leg.

He was crossing the street on his way back to the office when he spotted Marshal Beckmann coming out of the telegraph shack. Beckmann raised a hand in greeting and joined Sweet-water's lawman.

'What they have to say?' Tyree asked.

Beckmann fished a cigar from his coat and stuck it in his mouth. He lit it with a match, taking his time.

'They want me to ride on over to Madison. Some trouble brewing between the local cow outfits. Been a couple of shootings already.'

'That it?'

'Yes. Sorry, Sam, but no news about Jim Travis.'

'Damn!' Tyree said. 'Where the hell is that boy?'

Beckmann shrugged. 'He seems to have disappeared. We know he went into Mexico. There have been rumours he trailed the Parsons bunch back over the border but we can't be sure. If they all did get back on our side it may have been further east, and that would put them in Apache country.'

They reached the jail. Tyree climbed the steps and settled himself in his cane-backed chair.

'It's been too damn long,' he said.

Beckmann didn't answer and Tyree glanced at him. The marshal was looking along the street.

'I'll be damned,' Beckmann said softly.

'What?'

Tyree took a look himself.

And saw Jim Travis riding up the street towards the jail. Jim had another horse on a lead rope. There was a rider on the second horse. His feet were tied in the stirrups and his hands roped to the saddlehorn. Both men were caked in dust. Their clothing was filthy, almost in rags. Beneath the thick growths on their faces were dark bruises and part-healed cuts. Although it was difficult to identify the second man Tyree knew it had to be Luke Parsons.

Jim reined in and climbed down off his horse. He took a set of saddlebags and placed them on the steps just below where Beckmann was standing.

'Sam, he's all yours,' Jim said, indicating the man on the second horse.

'You all right, Jim?'

'I'm fine, Sam.'

From what Tyree could see Jim was far from being fine. He looked dog-tired. At the limit of his endurance.

'There's a spare cot in back of the jail,' Tyree said. 'Jim, why don't you use it. We can talk later. Any time you're ready.'

'Sounds like a good idea.'

'I'll take care of our friend here,' Beckmann said, indicating Luke Parsons. He walked by Jim, saying: 'You made it, Jim Travis. Welcome home.'

'Sam, you hear anything about John Mulchay?' Jim asked.

'He's doing fine. You saved that man's life, Jim. Last message I had from him said to tell you he expects you to visit first chance you get. And so does Jenny.' Tyree smiled. 'Appears you've been a trifle busy since you left Sweetwater.'

Jim nodded. 'Some,' he said. His reply expressed a great deal of what he was thinking, and what he'd been through.

Behind Jim the street was beginning to fill as his return was noticed. In ones and twos the people of Sweetwater began to gather.

'Hey, Travis, looks like you got 'em.'

Jim turned at the call. He faced the growing crowd, his face expressionless. Among the spectators were many of the men he'd argued with the night before he'd ridden out. Jim felt a growing resentment. Here they were. The ones who had let him ride off alone. Not one of them had shown enough guts to go after what was rightly theirs.

'Jim, did you get the money back?' someone yelled from the body of the crowd.

Jim turned his back on them.

'Well did you, Travis?'

Jim recognized Henry Sutton's voice instantly. He spun on his heel and watched the banker of Sweetwater elbow his way through the crowd.

'I asked you a question, boy,' Sutton snapped.

'Well I don't feel I have to jump,

Mister, just because you decide to bark. I don't work for you, Sutton, and I damn well don't owe you a thing.'

'Now look here, Travis . . .'

'No. *You* listen to me,' Jim said. 'I went after Parsons to get *my* money. Not for the bank. Or for you. Or for anyone else in this town. Nobody wanted to know me when I looked for help.'

'I still have a right to know where the bank's money is,' Sutton demanded.

'The hell you do, mister.'

Sutton looked to Tyree for help. It wasn't forthcoming. Sweetwater's sheriff was watching the procedings with interest, and a trace of amusement.

Marshal Beckmann had released Luke Parsons from his horse and was leading him to the jail. As Parsons started up the steps to the boardwalk he kicked the saddlebags holding the money down onto the street.

Henry Sutton glanced at the bags, then at Parsons, who gave a knowing grin before Beckmann hustled him out of sight.

'It's in there,' Sutton said. 'The money's been there all the time.'

He started forward, reaching for the saddlebags.

'Keep your hands off those bags,' Jim said softly, keeping his voice down so that only Sutton and Tyree could hear.

It was the hard edge to Jim's words that made Tyree sit up and take notice. He realized that Jim was close to the edge. If Sutton persisted Jim might easily hit back.

'Henry,' Tyree said evenly, rising from his chair, 'leave it for now. Just back off and let me handle things.'

'You heard what he . . . ' Sutton blurted out.

Tyree stepped down beside Jim, touching him on the arm. 'Take the bags inside my office, Jim, and we'll sort all this out.'

Jim nodded. He picked up the bags and walked for the jail, just ahead of Tyree.

'You came that close, Henry,' Tyree said. 'If anything had happened I'd have found it hard to blame Jim for any of it.'

He followed Jim into the jail and closed the door behind him.

'Give me those damn bags,' Tyree said. He took the saddlebags and dumped them in a corner of the office. 'You get it all back?'

'Far as I know,' Jim said. He unbuttoned his shirt pocket and pulled out a thick wad of notes. 'I took mine out.'

'I'm damned sure you did. I'll hand the rest back to Sutton. In my own time. Let him sweat a while first.'

'Is that offer of a bed still open?'

'Sure. Go ahead.'

'I'll rest up a while,' Jim said. 'Then I'm heading out, Sam Got my money and I've got a place to go now.'

'The Mulchay place?'

'I reckon.' Jim smiled. 'Got a few things to say to someone. If she'll listen.'

'I think she will,' Tyree said.

He watched Jim vanish through the door leading into the rear of the jail.

Tyree busied himself with a few items of business. Beckmann returned from the cells where he'd locked Parsons up.

'I'll go talk to the boys out there,' the marshal said. 'Tell them their money's safe.'

Tyree nodded. He took a walk through to the rear of the jail and had a quick look at Parsons. The outlaw was stretched out on his bunk, staring at the ceiling. Before he went back to the office Tyree looked in on Jim. The door of the small room was open. Jim was sprawled across the low cot. He hadn't even bothered to take off his boots or gunbelt. He was already in a deep sleep. His right hand hung over the edge of the cot. Most of his three thousand dollars had slipped through his fingers and lay on the floor. Tyree stepped into the room. He crouched beside the cot and began to pick up Jim's money.

It was, he decided, the least he could do.

We do hope that you have enjoyed reading this large print book.

Did you know that all of our titles are available for purchase?

We publish a wide range of high quality large print books including:
Romances, Mysteries, Classics
General Fiction
Non Fiction and Westerns

Special interest titles available in large print are:
The Little Oxford Dictionary
Music Book, Song Book
Hymn Book, Service Book

Also available from us courtesy of Oxford University Press:
Young Readers' Dictionary
(large print edition)
Young Readers' Thesaurus
(large print edition)

For further information or a free brochure, please contact us at:
Ulverscroft Large Print Books Ltd.,
The Green, Bradgate Road, Anstey,
Leicester, LE7 7FU, England.
Tel: (00 44) **0116 236 4325**
Fax: (00 44) **0116 234 0205**

NEVADA HAWK

Hank J. Kirby

The long trail ended at Castle Rock in New Mexico Territory. Nevada found the man who had murdered his wife — then killed him as he'd planned. What was the next step now? A talented gunman like Nevada was always in demand. He didn't care what type of work he took on, or how dangerous. Life — his own, that is — no longer mattered much any more. Or did it . . . ? He would breathe plenty of gunsmoke before he found the answer.

BRIGHAM'S WAY

Richard Wyler

Brigham, Seth and Jacob Tyler came to the Colorado badlands in search of gold. They found it alright — but they also found it took a deal of holding onto. There were violent killers ready to take it from them . . . and the three brothers would have to match bullet for bullet for each of them to retain his wealth, and forge his own way in life.